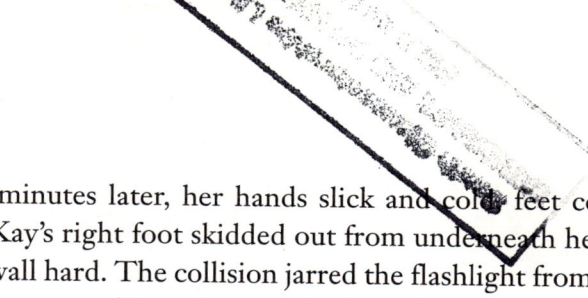

Ten minutes later, her hands slick and cold, feet completely numb, Kay's right foot skidded out from underneath her and she hit the wall hard. The collision jarred the flashlight from her hand and it disappeared into about ten inches of water. She plunged her hands into the frigid water, frantically searching for the flashlight. The water was dark and deep and her hands came up empty. "Tory, the water. It's still rising. We need to find higher ground. Now!"

Tory stopped and turned. For a moment, they didn't move or speak. The only sounds were of running water—a trickling, pooling sound that seemed to come from above, below, all around them. It was dripping on their faces, swirling around their calves. Tory felt for Kay's arm and gripped it firmly. "Stay close. I should've listened to you before. Damn!"

Visit

Bella Books

at

BellaBooks.com

or call our toll-free number

1-800-729-4992

Love Speaks Her Name

Copyright© 2004 by Laura DeHart Young

Bella Books, Inc.
P.O. Box 10543
Tallahassee, FL 32302

All rights reserved. No part of this book may be reproduced or transmitted in any form or by any means, electronic or mechanical, including photocopying, without permission in writing from the publisher.

Printed in the United States of America on acid-free paper
First Edition

Editor: Anna Chinappi
Cover designer: Sandy Knowles

ISBN 1-59493-002-3

For Colleen and Tracie

When memories are my evenings, they will be of you . . .

About the Author

Laura DeHart Young was born in a small town in New Jersey—so small and obscure that she now lies and says she is a native Pennsylvanian (where she did live for over twenty years). No wonder she moved to the metro Atlanta area of almost four million people seven years ago to enjoy a vastly different living experience. Now she yearns for vacations in the north Georgia mountains where there is no traffic and far fewer people.

When not writing and working for a technology company headquartered north of Atlanta, Laura collects famous autographs (Lucille Ball, Paul Newman, Elizabeth Taylor, Sally Field just to name a very few) and dabbles in digital photography. She also loves travel, attending LPGA golf tournaments, reading, spending time with family, gardening, staring at her freshwater aquarium, and relaxing in the beautiful sunroom of her new home.

Laura's constant companion for the past thirteen years has been her pug, Dudley. And, oh yeah, her partner of seven years, Jerri.

Chapter One

Kay Westmore had come to view her life as time interrupted by defining moments. The interruptions were like rooms in a house where she wandered, lingering over memories and lessons learned. In one room was her life before Lela Newlin, her partner of two years, when she struggled with failed relationships and loneliness. In another room was life before the death of her mother when existence seemed centered and held together by the strong will of her mother's personality. There were other rooms holding memories of jobs and the people connected with them or circles of friends now broken and scattered. As the minister continued reading from the Bible in a somber tone, Kay ran her fingers along the smooth dark wood of her father's casket, knowing there would be a new room now holding safe the joyous memories of him.

On a warm July day in Fairbanks, along the banks of the Chena River, the time to say good-bye to her father had come. Her father had died at the age of 76 from complications of Parkinson's, a disease he battled for more than twenty years. The disease had ravaged his body and, finally, his spirit. The last time Kay visited her father, his eyes were yellowed from medication, his will to fight gone. His body was broken and bent, speech slurred, mind sometimes frightened by paranoia and confusion. Voices unheard by others tortured him and there were times when Kay was uncertain whether or not he knew her. This was no longer a man she recognized either, was not the father who drove their family to Canada during summer vacations, and worked thirty-five years for the federal government, never missing a day of work due to illness. The father who, on his hands and knees, scrubbed the kitchen floor when her mother was pregnant with Julie, washed the dishes after dinner, vacuumed the carpets, dusted the dining room furniture. There was nothing he wouldn't do for them—or hadn't done.

After the graveside service, as Kay cradled the American flag that had adorned her father's casket, she recalled turning to Lela during the service and declaring, "I have no parents now." The thought had hit her suddenly and she felt a surge of panic. She and her sister were all that remained of a once happy family. At the age of forty, she was left spinning on her own axis and it frightened her. For most of her life she was estranged from her younger sister, Julie. In recent years they had formed a tenuous bond. But with the loss of both her mother and father came a loneliness and isolation she never experienced. Memories sustained her now—Mom's steady voice on the phone, Dad's staccato greeting and warm smile, his unsteady hands clutching a fluttering newspaper.

A throbbing pain behind her eyes signaled a nasty headache as Lela's truck sputtered noisily down the Fairbanks road from the cemetery. The truck backfired twice, jostling Kay roughly in the back seat. Lela drove the truck and Alex Chambers, Kay's best friend of many years, was riding shotgun. Alex said something about the truck and Lela shrugged. Kay couldn't make out the words because the pulsing behind her eyes now pounded in her ears. Kay buried her face in the triangular folded flag and cried. The fabric felt coarse against her cheek and smelled like new bed linens. Clutching the flag transported her to another moment as she sorted through her mother's clothing, deciding what to discard and what to donate to charity. The fragrance of her mother's perfume, still clinging to her dresses and nightgowns, made the terrible loss very real—as did the flag she held tightly against her chest.

A week later, after settling her father's affairs in Fairbanks, Kay and Lela returned to Anchorage where they now lived. They moved to Alaska's largest city a little over a year ago after Kay changed jobs with the Department of the Interior. A new administration in Washington had ended her four-year tenure as director of the National Park Service. A new director was hired but because of Kay's reputation in government circles, she was asked to take the position of director of Denali National Park and Preserve, Alaska's last wilderness frontier. With more than six million acres of majestic mountains, calving glaciers, and rugged forests, the park was located two hours north of Anchorage. Kay made frequent trips to the park, sometimes staying for days or weeks. But her home office was located at the National Park Service regional headquarters in downtown Anchorage.

Lela parked the truck in the driveway of the cedar ranch that had become their home. With a view of the Chugach Mountains, the house sat a short distance from a private road on four acres, nestled in the shadow of the mountain range. The jagged snow-covered peaks pierced the blue heavens and dominated the landscape with a power unmatched in nature. The house, with its four bedrooms and three baths, was a spacious and tranquil retreat. One of those bedrooms and baths was located at the rear of the house, where Alex lived. A little more than a year ago, Alex and her longtime partner, Pat, had called it quits after thirteen years. Six months later, Alex was diagnosed with breast cancer. Knowing that her friend faced a rigorous cycle of chemotherapy, Kay returned to Fairbanks to collect Alex and her belongings.

The cancer announced itself daily. Alex had amassed a large collection of baseball caps to cover the hair loss caused by powerful drugs Kay could not pronounce. Today's selection was a khaki cap with *Anchorage* embroidered across the front. The one activity that kept Alex's spirits elevated was her longtime hobby of cooking. After the three-hour trip from Fairbanks, Lela and Kay were content to sit at the kitchen table and observe Alex's mastery in the kitchen. Normally on a Saturday night, they ventured downtown for dinner if Alex was feeling up to it. But exhaustion from the trip and the strain of recent weeks erased any thoughts of leaving the house. When Alex offered to cook dinner, it was a welcome relief. Soon she was preparing Alaskan halibut with a chipotle pepper and honey glaze. Mangos were being chopped for mango chutney. It was one of Kay's favorite meals.

Kay refilled Alex's iced tea glass and absentmindedly leaned over, kissing her cheek. "What did I do to deserve my favorite dinner?"

The brim of the cap shadowed Alex's face, but Kay caught the hint of a smile. "It would take me too long to answer that question. So just sit down and enjoy it."

Kay grinned and snatched a beer from the refrigerator. Sitting down at the kitchen table, she kicked off her LL Bean all-weather boots and watched her friend as she finished dicing the mango. Alex stopped working for a brief moment, took a deep breath, and sighed heavily. Kay noticed Alex's shoulders sag. "You okay?"

Alex didn't turn around. She started to chop again and said, "There was a message on my phone from Pat. Apparently she's heard about my diagnosis. I visited with a few friends while we were in Fairbanks and it doesn't surprise me that word's gotten around."

Kay glanced at Lela who was sipping tea and reading the morning paper she'd rescued from the front porch. "What did she say in the message?" Lela asked. Their collective shock must have been apparent because Alex laughed.

"It's okay you two. I haven't fallen apart or anything. The message was brief. She called to find out how I'm feeling. Said she heard the news and is very concerned. Wants me to call her back." Alex turned toward them and shrugged. "I expected this sooner or later."

"You going to call her?" Kay asked.

"Not if it means calling her at her new girlfriend's house. I suppose I could call her at work. But I'm not really excited about the idea, if you want to know the truth."

While Kay was able to understand Pat's concern, the fact that Pat called Alex infuriated her. Alex had been through enough torture. Finding out that Pat recently moved in with her new girlfriend must have been brutal for Alex to hear. "She's living with Sheila now? When did that happen?"

"Near as I can figure out she's been there about three weeks." Alex threw her iced tea down the drain and poured a glass of wine. "Our house sold pretty quickly so I guess she had to do something."

Lela's dark eyes look pained for their friend as she slid dinner plates onto the table and folded linen napkins into perfect squares. "You have so much to deal with right now, Alex. I think it would have been better if Pat had not called."

Alex leaned against the kitchen counter and sipped her wine. "Kay just lost a parent. That's what I've been dealing with." She wiped her hands on her apron, looking unconcerned. "I haven't really thought about Pat lately. At least not until I heard her message. I've been thinking about other things like helping Kay cope with her loss."

Kay was touched by her friend's words. For months, Alex endured chemotherapy treatments once every three weeks. After each round of drugs, she was sick for days, confined to bed and unable to eat. Dressed in a short-sleeved gray sweater and jeans,

Alex was thinner by about ten pounds. But her five-foot-six-inch frame still maintained its country-girl rugged look in spite of the demanding chemotherapy regimen ordered by the oncologist. The only other signs of illness were a slightly pale complexion and the ever-present baseball cap that hid the loss of her long auburn hair.

Dinner was quiet and Kay was happy for the beer buzz. Too much had happened—was happening. The thing with Al and Pat had blindsided her completely. Like any couple, Alex and Pat faced problems over the years but always worked them out. The two of them were total opposites and the way they kept their partnership alive and meaningful—full of laughter and sharing—always inspired Kay. When their breakup happened, Kay knew she would lose a friend in the process. It always happened that way. No matter how hard she tried to manage her way through the tidal wave of the breakup, she was constantly in the middle and it became impossible not to hurt one or the other. Eventually, she had to choose. Alex was in pain. If that wasn't enough, their history together went as far back as childhood. They were soul mates for what seemed like two lifetimes. Pat became a happy part of the equation later on, but there was always that special connection with Al. They grew up together in Fairbanks. In grade school they played kickball at recess and passed notes in class. In middle school they planned their lives, including husbands and children. In junior high school they discovered their sexuality and in high school they dated women, went to their first lesbian bar, came out to their families. Life had whipped them around its centrifuge until their experiences were forever mixed. *Chemotherapy.* The cumbersome word tumbled through Kay's brain like a fatal bullet. Kay could not imagine life without Alex. Until six months ago that possibility never entered her mind. But it was there now, a nagging whisper that persisted twenty-four hours a day—waking her in the middle of the night and leaving her in a cold sweat.

Lela's bare feet muffled her footsteps on the hardwood floor as she undressed. Kay watched as Lela moved across the room, her body softly lit by a bedside lamp. Her long dark hair was striking against the smooth features of her face and beige skin. Lela's heritage was Native American, as was her spirit. Her people were the Inuit, the original settlers of Alaska more than two thousand years ago. Lela served her people as lead attorney for the Bureau of Native Land Preservation, an organization formed by Native American tribes to halt oil, gas drilling, and mining in protected reserves. With the new administration in Washington, Lela and her people were fighting an uphill battle.

Lela snuggled against Kay's shoulder. "You are quiet tonight," she said, her voice breaking. "You are very sad and I am sorry."

"My father was suffering and for him I'm glad it's over. But I feel so mortal now. There's an emptiness inside that I've never known."

"Because your parents are gone?"

"Yes. It's made me think a lot about what I'm doing with my life. What I'll leave behind, if anything." Kay buried her face in Lela's hair, kissed Lela's forehead. She fought the lump forming in her throat. "All of these crazy thoughts have been crawling around my head, Lela. Maybe I'm starting to lose it."

Lela wound her fingers through Kay's hair. "It is a hard time for you. It is natural to question things."

"Maybe. But there's a part of me that's angry. Angry and hurt that my parents are gone. Furious at what's happening to Al. First Pat leaves her and now cancer. I'm sorry but that just sucks."

"But she seems stronger this past month. Don't you agree?"

"You don't know Al like I do. She's not a fighter. She's this peaceful worrywart who nurtures others. Taking care of others is her job and she's great at it. She's not great at letting people take care of her."

"We cannot change her, Kay. All we can do is be here for her."

"I hope that's enough."

During the month of July, days were twenty hours long in Anchorage. At night, the darkness was more like dusk—filled with murky shadows and a grayish horizon. By the time Kay got up for work at seven o'clock in the morning on Monday, it had been daylight for three and a half hours. At the office, Kay found lox, bagels, and cream cheese spread across the counter in front of Tammy's desk.

"Special occasion?" she asked Tammy, while snatching a Styrofoam plate.

"You're back," she replied sweetly. "We've all been worried about you."

"Thanks. That's really kind of you to say." Tammy was in her early twenties, divorced, and had a young son at home. She graduated from college a couple of years before while working nights and pretty much kept the office running.

"Your mail is sorted and on your desk," Tammy said with a demure smile. She poured Kay some coffee. "Your messages are on your desk, too. The ones I could call back, I did. But there are a few you'll want to take care of yourself."

"Thanks for handling everything so efficiently while I was gone."

She smiled again, but this time it was coy and almost flirtatious. "No problem. Anything for you, boss." Without taking a breath, Tammy continued in a stream of run-on thoughts. "Listen, you've got a visitor this morning. Already in your office. I hope that's okay. People can be awfully pushy. But it seemed important. Some people have that air about them, you know? They just go barging in without a care in the world."

Kay smiled and said, "Who is it?"

"I can't tell you."

"You can't tell me who's waiting for me in *my* office?"

"Well, I know it's your office, Kay, but I promised. So I better not tell."

With an indifferent shrug, Kay said, "Oh, hell. May as well start the week off with a bang. Not knowing who it is makes it all the more interesting. But I hope whoever it is doesn't mind if I eat a bagel while we talk. I'm starved."

Kay opened the door to her office and stood transfixed in the entranceway. A flood of memories came back to her. The inspection of the Alaskan pipeline in the dead of winter and a second trip into the National Petroleum Reserve two years later to investigate allegations that oil companies were illegally drilling in protected areas. From the first day she met Grace Perry to the last day they worked together almost two years ago, their relationship had been love-hate. But in retrospect Kay realized it had been the most exciting time in her career.

"Well, Miss Westmore, are you going to stand in that doorway forever?"

Kay stepped into the office and slid the cup of coffee and uneaten blueberry bagel onto her desk. So much for a quiet breakfast looking over budget reports. This was Grace's trademark—always arriving when least expected and never announced. "You like doing this to me, don't you?"

"Of course. Your reaction is always worth whatever travel adventures I've endured to get here." Grace got up and hugged her warmly. "I'm not your boss anymore so I can do this. It's good to see you, Kay," she said, patting Kay's back. "You look fantastic."

"So do you." Kay smiled at her former boss. Grace, now in her early fifties, was no less beautiful than when Kay first met her six years ago. The fair complexion, long auburn hair, and all-knowing smile that sometimes annoyed her, especially when Grace was in a mood, were the same. "Dare I ask what brings you from the intrigue of life in Washington to the wilderness of Anchorage? I'd like to think you came just to see me, but I simply can't convince myself."

"Kay, you're as amusing as I remember. Of course I'm here to see you." Grace sat down again, crossing her legs and letting a cream-colored leather pump dangle from her foot, as was her habit. "I also need your help with a project. But all of that can wait until I catch up with your news. What's been happening these past two years?"

Once Grace had a cup of coffee in her hand, courtesy of Tammy, Kay plopped down at her desk, now happy to push the work aside to reminisce. "Well, Lela and I live in Anchorage, as you know. We bought a beautiful house with a view of the mountains. We've got a friend living with us, too. Unfortunately, Alex is very ill but we're hoping for the best."

"Your friend Alex from Fairbanks? I remember her name. You spoke of her often."

"Yes. She was diagnosed with breast cancer six months ago."

"I'm so sorry, Kay." Grace reached out and squeezed Kay's arm. "I also want to say how very sorry I was to learn of your father's death. I wanted to be at the funeral, but my daughter and I were visiting family in Florida at the time."

"Please don't apologize. I got your flowers and your lovely note. I appreciated the kind words. How's your daughter?"

"Thirteen going on thirty. Knows absolutely everything."

"That's the age it starts to get fun with kids."

"It's an amazing process—watching her transform into a young lady before my eyes. There's nothing like it in the world."

"So, I hear you're a consultant in Washington," Kay said, leaning her elbows on her desk, studying Grace's cat-like eyes.

"Yes, well I have managed to make myself useful after my stint as Secretary of the Interior. They still call me madame secretary, you know." Grace smoothed the skirt of her perfectly tailored linen suit. "It amuses me to no end."

"If I called you that, you'd belt me a good one."

"I would. But I do love it when my political enemies are forced to kowtow. Not that I have many political enemies, you understand. But after six years in the Cabinet there are a few, I suppose."

Grace mockingly looked over her shoulder and laughed. "I miss having the Secret Service nearby."

"Washington is still a dangerous place."

"Because you don't always recognize your enemies."

"So what kind of consulting are you doing?"

"I've stayed in the environmental area. Right now I'm doing some work for the Senate's environmental subcommittee. Even the Republicans call me on the phone for consultation."

"That's a drastic turn of events."

"Hell, it's a damned miracle."

Kay and Grace laughed in unison. There was a knock on the door and then a familiar voice bellowed, "Here ya are havin' old home week and ya didn't even bother invitin' me."

Grace turned toward the door. "Mr. Bend, hello. Why am I not surprised to find you here in Anchorage?"

"Well, ya know, I just figure I'll follow Kay around until she gets sick of me."

Grace smirked and shook Russ's hand. "If it hasn't happened yet, I doubt it ever will. But then you two are a matched set."

Russell Bend was one of Kay's best friends. He had worked for Kay at the National Park Service headquarters in Fairbanks. When Kay became director at Denali, she hired Russ as deputy director. It was part of the deal. In addition to the fact that he made her laugh like no one else, Russ was one of the top environmental and land management gurus in the country.

Russ, a huge bear of a man, had a gentle but imposing presence in any room. "Hey, I even got my own office now with a view and everything."

"A view of the parking lot," Kay interrupted.

"Well, lucky you," Grace said with a chuckle. "You're moving up in the world, Mr. Bend."

"Yeah, it was bound to happen sooner or later. An office with a view of the parkin' lot ain't bad. I used to have a desk in an old file room at the park service."

Kay shook her head. "And he never filed a thing."

"Now that ain't so. I filed things in nice piles on the floor. So what are two ladies cookin' up? Whenever you guys get together in an office, there's bound to be trouble and I usually end up in the middle of it." Russ stroked his beard. It was deep brown, peppered with gray. "Are we goin' someplace where it's cold and dark?"

"I do have a reason for being here," Grace said, picking up her briefcase. "And it does involve both of you. But we'll save that story for tomorrow. Will the two of you have lunch with me?"

"Of course we will," Kay said.

"Good. I'm at the Hilton downtown. Come by around noon tomorrow. Now I'm off to check in and make some phone calls."

"You have a car, Grace?" Russ asked. "Can I drive you?"

Grace patted Russ's shoulder. "I'd forgotten what a gentleman you are. Thank you, but I have a rental car. Thanks for the coffee, Kay."

Once Grace left, Russ occupied the chair Grace vacated. "Hey, boss, this feels like déjà vu all over again. Say, I think I've said that before."

Kay shook her head and chuckled, tapping her pen nervously on the desk. "Just like old times, heh?"

"What's she up to? 'Cause as I live and breathe, she's definitely up to somethin'."

"She didn't say. It was all small talk. What I do know is that she's doing consulting work for the Senate's environmental subcommittee."

"Hey, now that could be somethin' really big."

"True. I heard through the grapevine that she was consulting on Capitol Hill, but the projects must be pretty hush-hush. I've called her a few times over the last couple of years and she wouldn't talk much about her new role. Whatever the reason she's in Anchorage, I can only guess it has something to do with Denali. Why else would she be knocking on this office door?"

"True. She'd still be in Washington driving other people nuts."

Kay rubbed her eyes. "I have to say Russ that I'm up to my eyeballs in stress. I'm not sure I can handle Grace Perry right now."

"I'm not sure anyone handles Grace Perry. You just try the hell to survive."

Kay threw her briefcase on the sofa and picked up the mail. She shuffled through it halfheartedly before heading into the kitchen. Alex was reading the newspaper and drinking a cup of tea.

"How was your day?" Alex asked, peering over the top of the paper, the brim of her Seattle Mariners cap bent backward. Her eyes were the color of robin's eggs as they softly probed Kay's mood.

"Okay for a Monday," Kay muttered through an exhausted sigh. "Though something extraordinary happened this morning. Is Lela home yet?"

"No. She called about an hour ago and said she'd be home around seven so that's when I'm planning dinner." Alex folded the paper, giving Kay her full attention. "What extraordinary thing happened? You look stricken for lack of a better word."

"Had an unexpected visitor at the office. Grace Perry."

Alex's face registered the shock she felt. "You've got to be joking. I should've known it was the Grace Perry look. I've seen it before."

"No joke. All the way from Washington, D.C."

"Good grief. Does this mean you're going to be sent into the wilderness again on some mission of espionage?"

"Well, I'm comforted that it's July and not January. Grace's timing has never been good for our wilderness treks. But why she's here and what it means, I can only wonder—at least until tomorrow at noon. That's when Russ and I will learn our fate. We're having lunch with her downtown."

Alex shook her head in disgust. She looked better today, Kay thought. She was dressed in blue jeans and a white short-sleeved shell. "She's trouble. Always has been. I know you respected her as a boss Kay, but I worried myself silly about what she'd get you and Russ mixed up in next. It's always been something to further her political power."

"True. But as challenging as it was, I did enjoy working for her. Who knows, maybe it's nothing. How was your day?"

"Good. I went food shopping. Cooking's the only thing that relaxes me. Although I did find another project." Alex grabbed Kay's arm and led her into the den. "Curtains for the den. What do you think?"

The curtains were sheer panels that brought elegance to the room without obscuring the majestic view of the mountains. "They're perfect."

"I've been searching the Internet for ideas. Then I found these on sale."

Alex had always basked in domesticity. She loved decorating, flower gardening, crafts, and any project that involved working around the house. Alex was on medical leave now and as reigning goddess of the house she seemed to have found her best medicine. The linens and towels were perfectly folded and stacked in the hallway closet, specialty soaps decorated the bathroom sinks, and fresh flower sprays filled the dining room with their beauty and fragrance. Kay pleaded with Alex to stop for fear she wasn't getting the rest she needed. But those pleas fell on deaf ears. "You need to rest more," Kay said softly, resigned to the fact that she had already lost the battle.

"You worry too much." Alex squeezed Kay's hand. "Stop it. I'm happy here and I'm doing exactly what I need to be doing to beat this thing."

"Asking me not to worry about you is like asking me not to breathe. But I'm glad you're happy here. We love you." Kay hugged Alex and kissed her forehead. "I love you."

"Yeah, I know. I'm just irresistible. Now why don't you help me with dinner? We'll make something special for Lela."

The smell of a wood fire, the condensation on a wineglass, the sound of light jazz and making love to Lela were all reminders of their first months together. There was something spiritual about their moments in the bedroom—at least that was what Lela said. For Kay, it was Lela's gentleness, her feminine submissiveness that was a turn-on. Kay was in control and she enjoyed the pleasure she gave to Lela who moved seductively beneath her, sighing deeply and nibbling Kay's earlobes. In a sort of repetitive mantra, Kay's name was uttered over and over and Kay whispered back, "I love you."

Maybe their moments together were ordained for Lela by the spirits of her culture, but for Kay they were motivated by a desire to reconnect, to reach for something she feared was slipping away. Lela, too, seemed to ache for Kay's touch, urging Kay with every motion of those soft, round hips. Kay pinned Lela's wrists against the bed and eased the latex strap-on deeper until Lela moaned and cried out, her orgasm tightening around Kay's slow, steady thrusts.

Lela rolled her body over Kay's and stared into her eyes. "Our spirits soar together, Kay. Like eagles riding the mountain wind."

Kay closed her eyes and felt gentle kisses against her neck, Lela's warm breath against her skin. When Lela's hand slipped between her thighs, she heard her own wetness and felt the growing pleasure from Lela's touch. Moving their hips together, they fucked each other simultaneously, Kay's thrusts matching Lela's until they came together. Lela kissed Kay and rubbed her breasts against Kay's nipples until Kay came again, her hand wrapped in Lela's hair, pulling Lela's kisses deeper into her mouth.

After making love for a second time, their bodies lay intertwined, Lela's herbal-scented hair matted to the side of Kay's face.

"Kay," Lela whispered. "What you do to me."

"I hope I never lose the touch."

"That will never happen."

Kay kissed the top of Lela's head and closed her eyes, happy for the moments together. Lately, their time together had been limited by Lela's job and her frequent trips to Juneau where she filed most of the legal cases on behalf of the Bureau of Native Land Preservation. When Lela wasn't traveling, Kay was often away, sometimes for weeks at a time assessing the various campsites and tourist services offered by the Park Service across the vastness of Denali's great wilderness. When they were both at home, it was the spirituality of their relationship that seemed to reunite them. Walking hand in hand down by the inlet and talking for hours by firelight was how they reconnected. But the many days they spent apart each month had caused a strain on their relationship and Kay felt it. Lela was silent on the subject—as she often was—holding firm to the belief that the strength of their love would overcome all obstacles.

"You are leaving for Denali later this week?" Lela asked, encircling Kay's fingers with her own.

"That depends on why Grace is here. I need to find out what that's all about first. My original plan was to leave on Thursday."

"I hope Grace does not have some wild adventure arranged for you. I worry enough about you as it is. Roaming around Denali is dangerous enough on its own without Grace Perry's influence."

"Whatever Grace wants, she's here at the request of some very powerful people in Washington. Grace may have lost her job heading up the Interior office after the last election, but she solidified her reputation by exposing some very real threats to the environment. It left a lasting impression with a lot of people."

"I guess it was too much to hope that Grace would retire after leaving the Cabinet."

"Now, now. Remember, if it weren't for Grace, we never would have met."

Lela wrapped her arms around Kay's waist. "You had to remind me."

"Fair is fair."

"Call me tomorrow after your meeting with Grace."

"You'll be the first person I call."

Kay and Russ met Grace at noon on Tuesday in the lobby of the hotel expecting to head straight to lunch. Instead, they ended up in Grace's suite, huddled around the coffee table. Papers were piled and strewn throughout the room, along with maps and charts. Books were stacked on the desk and two laptops were powered up—one on the desk and another on the floor.

"Lunch will come later," Grace said firmly. "What I need to talk to you about must be discussed in private. But the mini bar's open. Can I get you anything to drink?"

Kay shot Russ a questioning look, and then they each accepted a soda. Russ began stroking his beard and shaking his left foot, both nervous habits.

"Well, I won't beat around the bush any longer. I know you're both wondering why I'm here. I mentioned to Kay that I've been working as a consultant for the government. Specifically the United States Senate's subcommittee on the environment." Grace slid some file folders from her briefcase. "This committee oversees Superfund sites, clean air legislation, land preservation, and a great deal more. They also monitor the pollution caused by industry, including mining operations due to the high environmental pollution involved in mining activities." Grace unfolded a map and Kay instinctively flinched. It was a map of Denali.

"There's no mining in Denali, Grace," Kay said confidently.

"Not in Denali, but just outside of Denali," Grace responded in a familiar and dismissive tone. "Right here."

Kay leaned closer to the map. Grace's finger was pointing to Sugarloaf Mountain, just northeast of the Nenana River. The river formed the eastern border of Denali. "Of course you know that Sugarloaf isn't within our jurisdiction, Grace."

"No matter. I have a blank check from the Senate to investigate that area and now I'll tell you why. But everything I say from this point on is classified." Some photo identification cards were slid across the table. "You've been cleared to hear this information. I've had you both subjected to extensive background checks. Hope you don't mind."

"Not at all, Grace," Russ said, obviously annoyed. "Just consider our lives open books."

"Remember the benzene, Mr. Bend?"

"Sure do."

"What I'm about to tell you makes the benzene scare seem trivial. Do you know what's being mined by the Sugarloaf Valley Mining Company?"

Kay shook her head. "Don't have a clue. I didn't even know there was a mining operation there."

"Recently the President called for greater research into fuel cell technology, which relies on platinum to create electricity without pollution. In fact, they're planning on spending a little more than one billion dollars to develop hydrogen-powered vehicles."

"So Sugarloaf is mining platinum?" Kay asked. "For the government?"

"Essentially, yes. The Sugarloaf Valley Mining Company was incorporated last year after securing a large contract with the Feds. You may know that the main sources of platinum in the world comes from mining operations in Alaska, Russia, and South Africa."

"So what's the problem?" Russ asked.

"The mine is being run by a French Canadian company, but the investors are mostly Saudis. That fact's not really too surprising. What's surprising is some intelligence that's come to the Senate via the CIA. That there may be more than platinum coming out of that mining operation—or at least out of that area."

Kay was confused. "Like what?"

"Uranium."

Russ's jaw dropped. "How's that possible?"

Grace leaned back in her chair and took a sip of bottled water. "To mine just a small amount of platinum, you have to process tons of ore. Alaskan ore is rich in uranium. A month ago, an Inuit fisherman who lives just north of Sugarloaf and fishes the Nenana River took ill."

"Radiation poisoning?" Kay asked.

"Exactly. He was taken to a local clinic. They didn't have the resources to help him so he was flown here to Anchorage."

"Could the radiation poisoning have been caused by any other source?" Russ asked. "The Inuit are a very nomadic people."

"Perhaps, but unlikely. The CIA sent an agent to the area. The agent is still there but needs assistance from survival experts who know Alaska, who understand this kind of terrain."

"What does a CIA agent need us for?" Russ asked. "Hell, they have access to the best training in the world."

"The agent needs a good cover, which you can provide, in order to get closer to the mines without arousing suspicion. More importantly, the agent also needs people who know this area, this land, and how to navigate its dangers. You are both highly qualified survival experts."

"But as Kay mentioned, it's not our area," Russ countered.

"Neither I nor the Senate of the United States really care about technicalities, Mr. Bend. Do some surveying. Some biological study of the river. I don't care what you devise as an excuse to be in that locale."

Kay shook her head in disbelief. "This is insane, Grace. We may know the terrain and we may be survival experts, but we aren't CIA agents. I'm sure we can devise some excuse, as you say, and provide cover for this agent. But then what?"

"That's a fair question. But here's the other piece of information you need to know. A source of uranium has been finding its way to some dangerous governments unfriendly to the U.S. There have been several previous attempts to trace its origins—all unsuccessful."

"What do you mean, unsuccessful?" Russ asked warily.

"The CIA has lost agents. Not in Alaska but in other regions of the world. What's been learned is enough to indicate that the source of the uranium is somewhere in Alaska. The fisherman's radiation poisoning near the Nenana River is an important clue—I'm certain of it."

"I don't like it, Grace. I'm sorry. It's way beyond our scope and experience," Kay argued.

"I disagree. You're both perfect for this assignment. You both work in Denali. The park entrance and main ranger station are located right on the Nenana River just twenty miles south of where the Inuit fisherman lives. It's a perfect setup to provide cover and resources for our agent."

"Fine," Kay said curtly. "But what are we to tell our boss?" Kay and Russ both worked for the National Park Service Director Connie Huntington.

"Unfortunately, you can't tell Connie anything. I'm hoping the two of you can devise reason enough to spend some field time near Nenana."

Kay tried to steady herself for the next question and answer. "When are you asking us to go?"

"As soon as possible without arousing suspicion with Connie or anyone else. I'll give you the final details tomorrow. I'll stop by your office in the morning."

Later that same afternoon, after a quiet and subdued lunch with Grace, Russ and Kay huddled back at the office digesting the news. Russ paced in front of her desk, lumbering back and forth like a grizzly bear and in just as foul a mood.

"Listen, part of me can respect Grace for all she's done to serve this country, but I hafta say, I think that dame's finally lost her mind. I've heard some pretty crazy shit from Grace over the years but this tops everything," he complained. "Uranium. Right out of Alaska and over to some unidentified enemy. And people are dyin' tryin' to find out how it's gettin' out of this region and where it's goin'."

"Let's face it, Russ. The nuclear threat from rogue countries is very real and there's a hell of a lot of uranium ore in Alaska. And I don't think they send CIA agents to the Nenana River as a matter of routine."

"So we've gotta go."

"Yeah, I think we do. As much as I'm against it—I suppose Grace was forced to find two people she had absolute trust in. Who else would she have gone to but us?"

"How long do you think we'll be gone? I'd like to tell my wife somethin', even if it is a pack of lies."

"I'm thinking we can leave next week. That'll give you time to get the supplies we need. It'll also give me time to get the final details from Grace, plan our route, and contact Connie with some story about why we'll be out in the field for a couple of weeks. We were supposed to evaluate the campgrounds for upgrades in the fall. You've already started on the Riley Creek campsite, and I've been putting off the rest of the site evaluations for other priorities. But finishing these campsite evals is just the cover we need for Connie. While she assumes we're in Denali, we'll actually be heading to Sugarloaf."

"That oughtta work."

"Let's take a look at the map, Russ."

Russ unfolded a topographical map of Denali and spread it across Kay's desk. "We can take George Parks Highway to the park entrance."

"Exactly. We'll check the roster and see who's on duty at headquarters. Tell them we're doing the campground inspections and make like we're headed to Riley Creek. But then we'll go east to the river where a kayak and some equipment will be waiting for us. Well hidden."

"I'll take care of the supplies. If I order 'em today, we can take 'em up on Saturday and store 'em in the ranger shed at Riley Creek. We gonna take the river up to Sugarloaf?"

"That's right. There's too much tourist activity along the highway. Then there's the Alaska railroad. It's high season for tourists and I don't want to attract a lot of attention. It'll be much quieter on the river. I'm going to disagree with Grace on one point—other than whatever nonsense we tell Connie, our 'cover' near Sugarloaf will be the 'cover' of not being detected. We can't just prance around the Sugarloaf Valley Mining Company in our ranger uniforms and expect questions won't be asked. As I tried to tell Grace, it's not within our jurisdiction and we'll be noticed if we do a fool thing like that. Better not to be seen at all."

"You said it. That was a lame idea if I ever heard one."

"What time's sunset about now?"

"Just after eleven thirty p.m."

"That's when we'll put to water. That'll give us four and a half hours of darkness to get up the river to Sugarloaf."

"It's gonna be hell navigatin' the river in the dark."

"We'll manage. Now all we need to know is where we're hooking up with this CIA agent. But I suppose Grace will tell us that."

"I hope this person ain't a figment of Grace's imagination."

"Not likely. But what I do want us to remember is that someone inside the government is leaking information about agents who've been assigned to this case so far."

"Someone inside our own government's betrayin' CIA agents and sellin' uranium to rogue governments. Hell, I'm gonna call Tom Clancy and give him the lowdown so he can write his next book."

Russ left to make some phone calls and Kay slumped deep into her leather chair. She closed her eyes and replayed Grace's every word. Mining near Sugarloaf. She remembered something about mining east of Denali when she was with the Interior, but she couldn't recall the details. Kay reached for her desk phone.

"Lela, Russ and I met with Grace."

"And why is Grace Perry in Anchorage?" Lela asked in a weary voice.

At that very moment, Kay realized she had to lie. She cursed softly under her breath. It was all classified—every shred of information Grace had just told them. Kay couldn't tell Lela a damned thing about their assignment. "Uh, well, it's not all that bad." Kay struggled for the words to construct the lies she needed at that instant. "It's nothing but a routine trip into Denali. Some mines are leaking contaminants into the Nenana. Grace is working for the Senate environmental subcommittee and she wants us to slap the mining company's hands and make them play nice so a bunch of senators can feel important and powerful."

"And so Grace can feel powerful, too."

"That goes without saying. Personally, I think it's all hogwash, but we've got to check it out because some constituent friend of a senator stirred up trouble. No big deal. Just some water sampling, that's all."

"Why does Grace come to you with this request?"

"You know how Grace is. It's all about her reputation in Washington. If sending Russ and me on some meaningless errand results in more consulting jobs for Grace in the right government circles, I suppose these small favors are just as important as anything else to Grace."

Lela sounded confused. "Still, it is a long way for Grace to come to ask for water samples of the Nenana River."

Kay forced a laugh. "Hell, it may be that Grace is mellowing in her old age. I think she actually misses us."

"When do you leave to get these water samples?"

"Well, Russ and I need to evaluate some of the campgrounds for upgrades this fall, so we're going to combine that task with the Nenana excursion. That'll make both Connie and Grace happy at the same time."

"How long will you and Russell be gone?"

"A couple of weeks. If it's longer than that, I'll let you know. Nothing to worry about."

"Whenever Grace is involved, I will always worry."

Kay was still wilting under the stress of Grace's news yesterday and being forced to lie to Lela. Wednesday the stress continued with a tiring morning in the office planning the details of the mission. Grace had breezed in and out for some additional counsel with both of them. Kay couldn't figure out Grace's mood. She seemed impatient and nervous. She jumped from topic to topic and made what seemed like dozens of phone calls, slipping into an unoccupied office for privacy. Kay remembered when Grace didn't know how to turn on a laptop, much less use one effectively. Now she fired e-mail after e-mail in between the phone calls and her conversations with Kay and Russ. If that wasn't enough, Grace demanded to see six different topographical maps of Denali and another six or seven of Alaska. Russ ran back and forth to the map file, growling complaints when Grace was safely out of earshot. The rest of his day was spent talking to suppliers—calling in favors so the shipments they needed for the trip would arrive by Saturday. Kay and Russ were to meet with Grace for a final briefing on Friday. During this meeting, Grace planned to give them the rendezvous information they needed to hook up with the CIA agent who was already waiting for them somewhere in the Alaskan wilderness.

All of the morning's events swirled in Kay's head while she sat nervously in the oncologist's office later that afternoon. Usually, she waited about twenty minutes before the nurse returned to take her back to Alex who was undergoing another round of chemotherapy. In an effort not to think about what was happening to Alex, Kay let the stress of the morning overtake her terror of that waiting room. She hated that place—the smell of it, the dark green carpet and gray walls. She hated seeing the people—all of them seriously ill—enter, one after the other, through that blasted office door. Initially it was the word *cancer* in the same sentence with *Alex* that frightened her—a fright that made her physically sick, although she hid that reaction as best she could. It was February when she first heard that awful sentence. Alex was in

Anchorage visiting Kay and Lela. They were sitting in the kitchen having a glass of wine after dinner. It was as if someone had thrown a brick through the window and hit Kay square in the temple, knocking her completely senseless.

"I don't know how to tell you this except just to say it. I've got cancer." And then Alex's blue eyes settled on Kay and she remembered her heart fluttering and a strange pressure in her chest. The blue eyes were glassy, brimming with fear. Kay would never forget that look in her friend's eyes.

"When? When did you find this out? What cancer?" Kay asked.

"Breast cancer. Last week. I'm having surgery on Monday."

Kay glanced at Lela just to be certain that someone else in the room was hearing the same horrid words. Lela took Alex's hand and held it tightly. And that's when Kay began to struggle, knowing she couldn't appear panicked, cry, or curse, couldn't overturn a kitchen chair or throw the brick that had rendered her senseless back into the darkness.

"Miss Westmore, you can go back and see her now."

Kay looked up at the nurse and then walked the familiar hallway leading to the room where Alex was hooked up to bags of drugs. Every step of that walk was a supreme effort, a time when Kay sifted through thoughts and words that seemed so terribly inadequate. They didn't comfort her, so how in the world could they comfort Alex. And so mostly she said nothing—nothing about the cancer or the drugs. Nothing about the panic that washed over her in continuous waves or the sweat—all from fear—that trickled down the small of her back. She simply leaned over and kissed her friend on the forehead and uttered some asinine phrase that made her hate the cancer even more.

"Hey, babe. You got the cute nurse today, I see."

"Yeah. Just lucky, I guess."

Kay pulled up a chair. Two bags of drugs dripped slowly into Alex's veins. "How you feelin'?"

"On the edge of sick. But I think I can make it home before all that starts."

"Not to worry."

"What's the news from Grace?"

"She was behaving strangely today."

"More than usual?"

Kay chuckled. "Good point. I don't know. This new project we're working on must be getting to her."

"What's the project? I want to hear about it. It'll take my mind off my queasy stomach."

"Not much I can tell you. It's all a big secret. But I wouldn't expect any less from Grace. She's a consultant now, you know. For both political parties in Washington."

"How did she manage that? I thought everyone hated her."

"Yeah, but there was respect mixed in with the hate. Plus it was pretty much a given that Grace knew her stuff. Now she's got Democrats and Republicans eating out of her hand."

"She's a piece of work. Is this new project dangerous?"

"No, not at all," Kay lied. The last thing Kay wanted was Alex worrying about her. "It involves Denali but it's not dangerous."

"Lela going with you?"

"No."

"Why not?"

"Someone's got to keep an eye on you," Kay said with a smile.

"Right. What trouble can I possibly get into? I'm bald and I've got cancer."

"You're gorgeous. And you're not going to be bald forever. What's more, the cancer doesn't have a prayer."

"You think?"

"I know."

"Seriously, why isn't Lela going with you? That's how you met. That last mission Grace Perry sent you on."

"Lela's committed to her new job. Traveling back and forth to Juneau federal court going head to head with the government is pretty time consuming."

"Important for her people, too."

"Yes. Personally, I think they're beating their heads against a brick wall, but you can't just surrender the Alaskan wilderness to oil drilling."

"It's their home, Kay. The land."

"Yes, it is. And we've pretty much made a mess of it."

On the way home from the hospital annex, Kay pulled the car over three times so Alex could be sick. *God why are you doing this, to Alex of all people? She doesn't deserve this.* Holding Alex's shoulders on the side of the road, Kay could feel a deep, internal shudder within her friend's body as the drugs waged war on the cancer and on Alex. Alex was pale, skin clammy to the touch when Kay finally helped her through the front door. Lying on the bed in her room, Alex perspired and shook, her body still retching against the drugs. Kay made her a vanilla milkshake, but Alex couldn't drink it. Until Lela came home, she sat with Alex, patting her forehead with a cool washcloth until, mercifully, she fell asleep.

When Lela pulled into the driveway, Kay was sitting outside on the top step drinking a beer. It was her third and she could finally feel numb. Lela took one look at her and knew it had been a hellish day.

"Kay, what has happened?"

"Today was chemotherapy day."

"Yes, I know. Is Alex okay?"

"It was terrible. I mean, it's always terrible. But this time it really knocked her down. She's asleep now."

"Good. She needs the rest."

"I'm going to get another beer. You want one?"

"Have you eaten anything yet?"

"I'm not hungry."

"I'll make us a little something. Come inside."

Kay grabbed Lela's arm and hung on for dear life. "Lela, what if she dies?"

"Kay, you cannot allow yourself to think like that. Alex needs you to be strong."

Kay hung her head. "Today was scary."

"Of course it was, darling." Lela sat down on the front step and cradled Kay in her arms. "Some things are left to the spirits, Kay. We have the gift of time to pray for Alex's healing."

Kay closed her eyes and prayed for strength. Her friends always told her how strong she was, how resolute and unyielding. But her friend's illness called for a strength Kay did not know. "This is cancer, Lela. What do your spirits know about cancer?"

"You are upset and need to eat something. And the drinking doesn't help."

"Now's not the time to lecture me," Kay snapped.

"That was not my intention."

"I'm sorry. I'm worried out of my mind about Al, and this thing with Grace Perry isn't helping. I hate the thought of leaving Al now. Grace's timing sucks."

"I will look after her. All will be well. If we need you, we will know how to find you."

Kay wasn't so sure. Cell phones didn't work in the mountains. She would be able to call Lela from a landline phone at the ranger's station at Denali's main entrance. After that, she would be out of touch. She would have no way of knowing if something happened to Alex—or anyone for that matter. And what if another court date was set in Juneau? Lela would have to go.

As if reading her thoughts, Lela said, "And if I need to go to Juneau, I will call Selena." Selena was a childhood friend of Lela's who also worked at the Bureau of Native Land Preservation. "She has already promised to help me."

Kay drained the last of her beer. "I should be here. It's just not right."

"Come inside and have dinner. We will work everything out."

Chapter Two

Grace was in a rotten mood when Kay and Russ arrived at her hotel Friday morning. She barely said hello as she ushered them into the suite. Kay uttered the usual pleasantries and received no reply.

Room service delivered breakfast. Russ loaded his plate with two bagels, cream cheese, a banana, and several slices of cantaloupe. Kay grabbed some coffee and a banana and took the seat across from Grace who ate nothing.

Grace succinctly laid out the last details of the trip. Kay and Russ were to meet with a government agent northeast of the Nenana River at the western base of Sugarloaf Mountain. Grace produced a map with the exact coordinates of the rendezvous point.

"I plotted this map myself," Grace said. "I distrust everyone I talk to about this uranium scare. The only way you're to communicate with me is with these BlackBerry messengers. I've set up a mailbox for us. Don't use a cell phone or radio. Just these."

Grace slid the small black units across the table. Russ picked one up and inspected it curiously. "This thing will never work out there."

"It will work," Grace replied. "Don't worry about that."

"Uh, we don't have any transmission towers in that area, Grace. Nothing to carry the signal. We couldn't use a cell phone even if we wanted to."

"It will work," Grace repeated. "I've taken care of it. Let's move on, please."

Kay glanced at Russ who shrugged. He shoved the BlackBerry in his pocket and picked up the map. Kay asked, "Who is the agent? What's his name?"

"I don't know."

"Isn't that an important piece of information?" Kay insisted.

Grace stared at Kay coldly. "It's not a piece of information you'll be privy to right now."

Russ stood, his face registering disgust. He leaned one hand on the back of his chair, the other shoved deep into his pocket. Kay grabbed his arm but he jerked it away. "We don't work for you anymore, Grace, but out of respect for your job right now and because we care about the country we're livin' in, we're puttin' our butts squarely on the line. And we aren't, how'd you put it—*privy* to information? We should be given every scrap of information you have."

"For your *information*, Mr. Bend, I'm trying to protect your ass. So kindly put it back in that chair."

The room crackled with tension until, a few moments later, Russ sat down. Small droplets of sweat trickled down the small of Kay's back. It was clear that Grace had learned something that was disturbing her deeply. But whatever it was, Kay and Russ would leave without knowing the name of their contact. "Tell us what you can, Grace. We leave on Wednesday and need to make as many advance preparations as possible."

Lines of fatigue creased Grace's face.

"Make sure you have enough supplies for at least two weeks for three people. The agent has already been placed. I can't tell you exactly when, but you'll be met at the rendezvous point sometime between Thursday and Saturday of next week." Grace took a long sip of water and pointed to the map.

"Large deposits of ore at the Sugarloaf Valley Mining Company—you'll see them throughout the main yard when you get close to the mines. We've been using air surveillance to observe the ore dumps. The interesting thing we learned from studying the photographs taken of the area is that the ore dumps are static. They haven't changed in months. Mining operations haven't ceased so where's the new ore being dumped or taken? We know it's not being added to the existing dumps. It's being transported somewhere for processing. We need to know where."

"They haven't been able to observe any movement or shipping from the air?" Kay asked.

"No. That's the damn mystery," Grace said, tapping the table deliberately with her pen. "How is the ore being moved, where is it being moved and processed?"

"Into uranium," Russ said, breaking his silence.

Grace nodded, and then suddenly shook her head. "Okay, I'm not supposed to tell you this. But it's not just uranium ore we're looking for. Not according to some new intelligence we've received."

"What is it, Grace?" Kay asked, resting her hand on Grace's shoulder. "What are we looking for?"

"I shouldn't have involved you in this," Grace said almost sheepishly. "But I need people I can trust completely." Grace flashed a look of helplessness. "You know how much I respect and value you both. But everything is in motion now and I can't stop it."

"It's okay, Grace," Kay said, slightly unglued at seeing Grace so rattled. "Just tell us what we're looking for."

"Not enriched uranium but yellowcake. Uranium oxide to be

exact. You probably know that yellowcake is a partially refined ore. Easy to ship somewhere else so it can be combined with fluorine and then converted into a gas and eventually used to create weapons-grade uranium. We think it's shipping to Africa where Middle Eastern countries are negotiating purchase. Now you know everything that I know."

Kay was stunned. Uranium ore was one thing. But yellowcake was far more dangerous with potentially devastating consequences.

"It's hard to believe that yellowcake is coming out of Alaska. But what's happening in the Middle East makes it clear that every clue and information source needs to be investigated."

Russ rubbed his eyes and sighed heavily. "Jesus, Grace. You were right. Benzene is nothin' compared to this."

"One more thing," Grace said, hesitantly. "It's not the Senate I'm working with on this project. It's the NSA and the CIA. As soon as the Senate environmental subcommittee realized the implications of what we suspected, the matter was turned over to national security. Because of my experience in the area of environmental terrorism, my consult duties were shifted as well."

"You're working for the CIA and the National Security Administration?" Russ asked in disbelief.

"That's correct."

"Any more surprises?" Kay asked.

"No. And I really don't know who the agent is who'll be meeting you near Sugarloaf. It's safer that way. Now I expect an update each day at five o'clock sharp. I better see an e-mail pop onto my screen from one of those BlackBerries—and not one second past that deadline. Is that clear?"

Kay picked up the BlackBerry messenger and turned it over in her hand. "Yeah, that's clear. You'll get your first message next Thursday when we've made our contact with the agent at Sugarloaf."

For many hours that afternoon, Kay sat at her desk staring at a map of the Nenana River, Sugarloaf Mountain, and the valley where the Sugarloaf Valley Mining Company was excavating. In addition to the platinum mine at Sugarloaf, there were two mines north of Denali and Sugarloaf—one that was still operational and one that was not. Eagle Pass Coal Mine had been in existence since 1918 and was one of Alaska's largest coal mining operations. The existence of this mine had resulted in the settling of Healy, a town of about 650 people. The second mining operation, Trapper Creek Mine, was located two miles east of Eagle Pass and was closed years ago for countless regulatory violations discovered by the Environmental Protection Agency. An old gold mine and later a coal mine, Trapper Creek was notorious for its unfair treatment of the Native American miners who worked the cramped tunnels below the earth. The same mining operation had also been fined for dumping waste materials and chemicals into the surrounding environment. Kay couldn't help but wonder if there was any connection between these two mines and the Sugarloaf area. Kay threw her pen down and reclined her chair. Tons of ore, old mines, illegal shipments of yellowcake out of Alaska—possibly to Africa. Two years ago it had been a benzene scare and threats from terrorists to contaminate the Alaskan wilderness with this highly lethal chemical. Now it was illegal uranium mining, which had all kinds of environmental implications, including groundwater contamination and radioactive runoff into lakes, streams, and rivers. Add to that the potential for enriching the uranium and creating nuclear weapons, and the threat of cataclysmic terrorism was all too real.

Kay picked up the phone and punched the numbers for her boss, Connie Huntington, in Washington, D.C. Somehow, Kay had acquired another boss of higher authority, and she was about to lie to Connie.

After exchanging the usual pleasantries, Kay launched into her proposal. "Connie, I've put together a plan to conduct those site visits you requested of the Denali park facilities, including the campgrounds and ranger stations. Russ has already been working at Riley Creek."

"Excellent, Kay. That's good news. Any budget estimates for Riley Creek yet?"

"I think we're looking at about one and a half million right now. That's if we install the sanitary dump station and pave the access road."

"You think we'll be in that range for the other sites?"

"Probably under. Riley Creek is in need of the most extensive rehab."

"Well, as you know, I need to include any site improvements or facility needs in next year's budget. When do you leave?"

"Next week. Russ and I figure about two to three weeks to complete the assessment."

"You'll keep me apprised?"

"Absolutely. You'll have a complete briefing when I return, along with a detailed report."

"Look forward to seeing your recommendations. By the way, your public relations efforts have resulted in a great deal of positive press for Denali and Alaska. Tourist numbers are up and our travel industry partners are happy. It's been a good summer season so far despite the rocky economy. Congratulations."

"Thanks, Connie."

At the front desk, Tammy was busy typing minutes from a recent staff meeting. Kay grabbed a paper napkin and wrapped it around a chocolate doughnut. "You keep bringing these doughnuts in and we'll all be on Weight Watchers by the end of summer."

"No one's forcing you," Tammy said, swiveling around toward Kay. "They're left over from this morning and probably stale by now."

Kay took a bite and reported, "Not that bad, actually."

"Why don't you go home and have a proper dinner?" Tammy scolded.

"I've got more work to do. Say, where's Russ?"

"Well, after he ate *two* stale doughnuts, I heard him mumble something about going down to the loading dock to check on some crates that just arrived."

"Oh, okay."

"This morning he asked me to send three whopping bills for supplies to Grace at her Washington address. She picking up the tab for our expenses now?"

"Just on some special items."

"Somebody said she's working for a senator."

"A bunch of them."

"Well, one thing's for sure, she's got you and Russ in a state."

"Is it that noticeable?"

"Yep, it is."

"Grace has a history of doing that. A history that had an ending two years ago. Or so we thought. Have Russ see me before he leaves."

"Sure thing."

"Kay, I need you to sign for some packages," another voice interjected.

Taking a bite of her doughnut, Kay turned toward the clipboard that had been shoved in front of her. "Ron, I thought you were in Denali checking into the bear problem at Savage Creek." Ron Hadley was the operations manager, a token job given to him by the previous director. Kay allowed him very little authority because of his inconsistent work habits. He was famous for calling in sick for days at a time.

"Got back this morning. Don't think there's much to the bear problem." Ron reeked of cigarette smoke. The pack of Marlboros in his left chest pocket was a fixture. "A couple of tourists missing some food, that's all."

"Are you sure?"

"Yeah I'm sure. Just some tourists hearing things go bump in the night. No big deal."

Kay eyed Ron skeptically. He was a thin man with unruly

brown hair and dark eyes that revealed little emotion other than complete contempt for Kay and her authority. He made no secret about the fact that due to his long tenure with the National Park Service at Denali, he should be park director. Kay was told that Ron suffered from angry white male syndrome. He believed that Kay's appointment was not based on merit but on the government's need to fill its quota of females in higher level jobs—at the expense of white males. Kay signed the shipping receipts. "What about the inventory projections for next year?"

"I'll be working on that next week. Anything else you want to know?"

The tone of the question was snippy and Kay was annoyed. "Not at the moment."

Ron sauntered toward his office and shut the door. Kay and Tammy exchanged looks of disgust. "Why do you put up with him?"

"If I fire him, he'll cause a big stink. I'm just not in the mood," Kay said, grabbing another doughnut. "Don't forget to send Russ my way."

About an hour later, Russ walked into Kay's office with a big grin on his face. "I love spendin' Grace Perry's money. That's the only satisfaction I've gotten out of this deal so far."

"We ready to go tomorrow?"

"Yeah. Everything's loaded in my truck. The truck's down in the garage and it'll be locked up for the night. My wife's pickin' me up in half an hour. We're meetin' at seven in the morning?"

"Bright and early. Listen, I've been studying the maps you pulled for Grace. North of Sugarloaf there are two mining operations. Of course there's the Eagle Pass Coal Mine. But do you remember Trapper Creek? Been closed for years now."

"Yeah. They got shut down for EPA infractions." Russ stroked his beard and stared thoughtfully at the ceiling. "I'm gonna guess about ten years ago. Nothin' but a crisscross of old tunnels under there now. All shut down and boarded up."

"You're right about the time frame. And from what I understand, it was originally an old gold mining operation. When the gold veins dried up, they started mining some coal. I think we should mention this area to the agent. Maybe there's a connection. Trapper Creek's not far from the Sugarloaf platinum mine and I can see where that mine might be overlooked."

Russ seemed distracted and kept glancing at his watch. "You got some hunch, boss?"

"Something like that. You need to be somewhere?"

"Gotta make a phone call before Jen picks me up. Listen, I've been studyin' those aerial photos of Sugarloaf Grace gave us. Went over those photos pixel by pixel. Ain't nothin' happenin' there that's bein' picked up by aerial surveillance that tells us where the new ore is disappearin' to. And Grace was right about those ore dumps in the main yard. Over the months those photographs were taken, those dumps are exactly the same. The bottom line is we need to see what's happenin' at ground zero."

"Agreed. I just hope this agent is a reasonable person. It's going to take a team effort to cover that terrain. And some luck wouldn't hurt either."

"Anyone who's workin' on a project with Grace, makes me nervous. By the way, she seems pretty jumpy to me."

"Grace?"

"Yeah. What do you make of it?"

"In my estimation, she feels like we've stumbled into something much bigger than she was originally briefed on. I think she's angry about that and regrets being pulled into this mess—and for pulling us along with her."

Chapter Three

The George Parks highway cut through some of the most beautiful terrain in Alaska. The highway traversed the park's eastern border and eventually ran parallel with the Nenana River. This Saturday excursion was meant to deliver supplies to the Riley Creek campsite. Russ and Kay would return to Anchorage later that evening knowing that their main supply cache was ready for next week's trip to Sugarloaf. Any last-minute gear and equipment would be packed in their backpacks when they left on Wednesday.

Russ chewed gum and tapped the steering wheel of his truck to the country music blaring from the radio. But Kay's attention eventually strayed from her human companion to the always breathtaking landscape. The Alaska mountain range was the foundation of the park's interior beauty. Its soaring peaks cut into the summer sky, out-dueling the heavens for majesty. Denali was a vast expanse of mountains, glaciers, taiga, and tundra. The forest was a combination of black and white spruce. Above the tree line the tundra began with its splashes of color, including the blue forget-me-not, Alaska's state flower. Rivers like McKinley and Nenana wound through the mountains hewing their own trails as if to say, "We are as mighty as you." The wilderness of Denali was forever changing and always in control. Roads only went so far and then stopped. Campsites were impermanent, vulnerable to the weather. Humans were temporary visitors in a land too wild to tame. In this place, nature ruled supreme.

Kay's focus drifted back to Russ who was attempting to drive with one hand and open a Pepsi with the other.

"Need help with that?" Kay offered.

"Naw. I do this all the time."

"I'm not surprised."

"Are you gonna nag me?"

"Have I ever?"

"Come to think of it, no. Now Grace Perry's another story. There's an art to nagging and she's mastered it. But it doesn't bother me much because I always have the sense that she knows exactly what she's doin' even if she's annoying the hell out of me."

"That's been true—at least in the past. But I worry that we're out of our league with this assignment."

Riley Creek campground was named for the creek that flowed east and then north past the main entrance to Denali and into the Nenana River. The campsite was within walking distance of the main park entrance and included accommodations for more than one hundred campers. It was the perfect site for stowing the gear Kay and Russ would need for the trip to Sugarloaf.

Russ drove the truck behind the main camping area to a large prefabricated storage shed used by park rangers. It took about thirty minutes to unload the truck of the two kayaks and other camping supplies. It took another thirty minutes to check and recheck the list. Once they were satisfied that nothing had been overlooked, Russ and Kay stored the gear out of sight in the back of the shed behind some old steel water barrels.

Russ was locking up the shed when Kay heard approaching footsteps. A female in a ranger uniform walked toward them. Though Kay knew many of the one hundred and fifty employees who worked for her, she did not recognize this one.

"Hey, there. How are you?" the woman said in a pleasant tone.

Russ dropped the ring of keys he was fiddling with and bent over to pick them up. Kay returned the greeting. "Hello. Kay Westmore. Nice to see you." Kay extended her hand and received a firm handshake in return.

"I recognize you from our all-hands meeting at the beginning of the summer in Anchorage. I'm Carla Grayson." Carla turned toward Russ who was still fidgeting with his keys. "Hi, Russ. Nice to see you again."

Kay quickly realized that the two must know one another since Russ had spent quite a bit of time in recent weeks conducting the site assessment at Riley Creek. "That's right. I'm sure you two have met."

Russ dropped his keys again. His face appeared flushed and he was sweating. "Hey, Carla. How's it goin' around here?" he asked in a subdued tone. He picked up the keys and finally reattached them to his belt loop.

"Everything's fine here, Russ. You need something from the shed? I've got the key."

"Oh, no. No. I was just lockin' it up. Wanted to see if we had enough room to store anything for the renovations once they get started."

"Maybe we should include a bigger storage shed in the renovation plan," Carla suggested with a laugh.

Russ smiled and then cleared his throat. "Sure. Why not?"

Carla took off her ranger's cap. The waves of her short blond hair rippled in the wind. "I installed those new towel dispensers yesterday. The ones you ordered for the restrooms."

"Oh, geez. That's great. Thanks." Russ turned to Kay, his eyes fixed somewhere above her head. "The old ones were busted."

At that moment, Kay sensed something was awry about their three-way meeting. She glanced at Carla who was looking at the ground, moving the dirt and gravel around with her boot. Carla seemed like a nice enough young woman—looked and acted very professionally for someone in her mid-twenties. But she, too, seemed nervous. Maybe Kay, the big boss from Anchorage, was making her nervous. Whatever the awkwardness, Kay shook it off. Maybe she was just sorry that Carla spotted them at the shed. Kay didn't want any of their equipment disturbed before she and Russ returned on Wednesday. It was unfortunate that their presence had been detected.

"Well, Carla. We're just here to take a quick look around," Kay offered as an additional cover-up. "It's been awhile since I've been here. Want to give me the grand tour?"

Carla smiled broadly. "Oh, I'd love to. Would you care for a cup of coffee first?"

"How about we have one after the tour."

Carla finished the campsite tour in about an hour and then made good on her promise of coffee. Kay and Carla sat inside the ranger cabin sipping the hazelnut brew while Russ paced in front of the building, finally sitting on the front steps perusing one of the tourist maps of Denali.

"Maybe Russ is planning a camping trip here," Kay joked.

"He knows this area like the back of his hand," Carla said. "Thought I knew Riley Creek until I met Russ. Then I realized I only knew about a quarter of the grounds."

"Takes time to know an area this size well."

"Not for Russ. Must come from experience. He knows Denali like no one else I've ever talked to. Every small stream—where it originates, the direction it flows. Every glacier and mountain peak. Where the moose and caribou graze. It's completely amazing."

Kay was uncomfortable and suddenly she knew why. There was an adoring tone that permeated every word Carla spoke concerning Russ. Kay became suddenly dizzy and thought she might pass out.

"You okay?" Carla asked. "You went kind of pale."

"Sudden rush of caffeine, I guess." Kay got up and steadied herself. "We've got to run. Lots more to do today. It was nice meeting you and thanks very much for the tour."

Kay opened the cabin door and slammed it behind her. The sound jolted Russ from his fake map reading. He got up and looked at Kay with a squinty-eyed grimace.

"Damn, you scared the crap out of me."

"Did I? So sorry. Let's get going."

In the truck on the way back to Anchorage, Kay maintained a steady stream of dialogue with herself. The commentary was like one monstrous run-on sentence without beginning or end. The words that peppered the commentary were hateful and judgmental of Russ as a person—or at least the person Kay thought she knew. Russ had always talked about his wife, Jennifer, like she was the center of his universe. They seemed inseparable in everything they did. Though they had no children, there was no lack of activity with extended family, yearly vacations, a joint love of fishing and sailing. It was a fifteen-year marriage between two high school sweethearts destined to be together. And now Kay's notion of this happily married and devoted couple had been reduced to bullshit in less than two hours. Kay could not sit still and was fidgeting even worse than Russ had with those damned keys back at Riley Creek.

"You got ants in your pants?" Russ asked, breaking the tension-laced silence.

"No worse than you did back at Riley Creek."

Russ took his eyes off the road. Kay could feel him staring at her. "What's that supposed to mean?"

"You know what it means."

"No, I don't. You been tossin' yourself around that seat ever since we left camp. That's what I'm talkin' about. I don't know what you're talkin' about."

"I'm talking about the affair you're having with Carla."

Russ slammed on the brakes and veered off the highway. "Are you nuts?"

"No. Are *you*?"

"She tell you that?"

"She didn't have to tell me. And you are way out of line."

"Are we talkin' as boss to employee or as friends?"

"Does it matter?"

"Yeah."

"Okay, we'll try friends first. Maybe we'll get somewhere. Like maybe you'll stop lying to me."

"Who the hell's lyin'? I ain't said nothin' yet."

"Well, consider this your turn to talk."

Russ scratched his beard, then smoothed it with his hand. He repeated this ritual twice before saying, "Okay, you're right. About Carla and me. Don't ask me to explain it 'cause I can't."

"How could you do this to Jennifer?"

"I said I can't explain it."

"How did it happen, Russ?"

"Shit, I don't know. How do these things happen? It ain't never happened to me before."

"What is she? All of twenty-five?"

"Twenty-four."

"Swell."

"Who are you to talk? Stef was way younger than you."

"True enough. But she wasn't an employee and I wasn't in a relationship."

"Are we back to boss and employee?"

"Yes we are because you've put us in a precarious position. You've left us open to a sexual harassment complaint. You are this woman's superior. And it has to stop now."

"She ain't gonna file no complaint."

"How do you know that? How do you know that when you finally come to your senses and end this thing, that she's not going to retaliate?"

"Because we love each other. She told me she'd quit the job if she has to."

"You're not making any sense right now."

"Talkin' to you ain't helpin' me."

"Then maybe we better get going."

Russ started the truck and screeched back onto the highway. He kept his eyes glued to the road and seemed deep in his own thoughts. Kay was still angry. Maybe betrayed was a better word. Who was this man sitting next to her? What had happened to her friend and colleague, Russell Bend?

When Kay arrived home, it was four o'clock in the afternoon. Lela's car was missing from the driveway, but Kay found Alex in the kitchen drinking a cup of tea. Her pale blue robe was wrapped snugly around her small frame and for the first time she appeared truly frail. There were dark circles under her eyes and her complexion had a pale cast.

"Hey, babe. How's it goin'?" Kay reached around Alex's shoulders and gave a gentle hug.

"I'm good. Just got up from a nap."

Kay sat down at the kitchen table and reached for an apple. "Where's the other lady of the house?"

"Food shopping and a couple of other errands."

"What do we have planned for this fine Saturday evening?"

"Don't know."

"Feel up for a ride? Maybe down to the inlet? Get some ice cream."

"Sounds great."

"Well, we'll wait for the old lady to get home. See if she'll chauffeur us."

Alex smiled. It was a welcome sight to see a hint of excitement creep back into those piercing blue eyes. "How did the trip to Riley Creek go?"

"It was a fascinating day, babe. I don't know any other way to explain it."

"Is that good or bad?"

"Some things are better left unsaid. But we accomplished what we needed and I suppose that counts for something."

About 300,000 people lived within ten miles of the Knik Arm of Cook Inlet—most of them in Anchorage. But the area was no less scenic because of its proximity to downtown Anchorage. Cook Inlet offered a spectacular view of the Chugach Mountains. Three nearby state refuges protected much of the inlet's expansive waterfowl habitat on the north shore. This time of year, the inlet offered spectacular views not only of the snow-capped mountains, but of the burgeoning population of beluga whales.

Kay, Lela, and Alex walked the edge of the inlet's north shore, enjoying the cool breeze that careened across the water and noisily rustled the brown grasses at water's edge. Alex locked her arm in Kay's, needing the steadiness to negotiate the rocky shoreline. It was not the first time Alex needed Kay's strength to remain steady. In fact, there were many times in the long history of their friendship when one of them deflected the blows meant for the other.

It had been raining for days, Kay remembered. Thunder and lightning kept her awake well into the early hours of the morning during that rain-soaked week in late March. On one of those nights, well after midnight, she finally began to drift into a light sleep, only to be awakened suddenly by a tapping sound at her bedroom window. She was fifteen years old and had her own bedroom, no longer having to share a room with her younger sister, Julie. The annoying tapping continued until Kay propped herself on her elbow and opened the window at her bedside. She stuck her head out the window and into the downpour, catching a glimpse of a shadow standing on the sidewalk bordered by evergreen bushes. The lightning streaked across the sky and the shadow became Alex, drenched to the skin, her breath visible in the cold night air.

"Al, what the hell are you doing?"

"Come down."

"It's after midnight. Are you crazy?"

"I need to talk to you."

Hearing the tremor in her voice, Kay threw on a pair of jeans and sweatshirt and managed to sneak outside without waking anyone.

When she met Alex at the side of the house, her nose was bleeding and her lip was swollen purple. Bleary-eyed, she stumbled into Kay's arms. "Had a fight with my mom."

Alex's mom was known for her drinking binges. Whenever Dolores Chambers opened a bottle of vodka or scotch, Alex was usually on the receiving end of the punishment that followed. The fact that she was an only child with divorced parents made Alex a vulnerable target of her mother's tirades. Alex's mother was born in Russia and fled to America just after World War II. Never comfortable in middle-class America, her mother brooded, drank, and flew into rages. Fed up with the drinking and constant abuse, Alex's father left when Alex was ten. More times than Kay cared to count, Al showed up at school with visible bruises like a black eye, bruised cheeks, and swollen lips. But there were a host of other bruises on Al's torso that only Kay knew about.

Kay hugged Alex gently and kissed her cheek. Her skin was

cold and wet. "Let's get out of the rain and then you can tell me what happened this time. C'mon back to the garage," she said, starting in that direction. "It'll be warmer in there and we can talk."

Kay put her arm through Alex's as she limped along stiffly, as if in pain. In the darkened garage, Kay dug out an army blanket from her father's old trunk. They sat on the metal trunk, huddled under the blanket. The musty fibers smelled like the garage—a mixture of oil and gasoline.

Pulling a rumpled tissue out of the pocket of her jeans, Kay wiped the blood from Alex's nose. "What happened?"

"She threw me out, Kay. I was in my room studying and I heard her in the kitchen. Heard the ice clink into a glass. I hate that sound. It gives me the creeps because I know what the night's gonna be like."

Kay put her arms around Alex's shoulders. She was still shivering. "What set her off this time?"

Her words came haltingly as Kay stroked her hair. "Don't really know. An hour after I heard her pour the first drink, she was in my room screaming about the house being a mess and that I was good for nothing. I told her I was studying and the next thing I know she's slapping me, punching me. I kicked at her and she grabbed my leg and pulled me from the bed onto the floor. Then she started hitting me with an old belt of my dad's."

"Bitch."

"She started screaming about hearing I was queer and that's why I never had any dates with boys. Someone told her that you and I were girlfriends."

Kay rolled her eyes. "That's all your mom and her drinking buddies have to do is gossip about their kids and wrecked marriages."

"I told her that I loved you. That really pissed her off. Told her I'm a lesbian and she spit at me. Then screamed at me to get out."

Kay gazed out the rain-soaked windowpane. In the glare of the backyard spotlight she could see that it was still pouring. Drops pelted the garage roof and the rush of water poured from the gutters just outside the door. "You know she'll sleep it off and be apologizing tomorrow," Kay offered lamely.

"Sure. Before she opens another bottle and then maybe kills me next time. I can't go home, Kay. Do you think I can sleep in here tonight?"

"In the garage?"

"Yeah, I'll be okay out here."

"Like hell you will. You can sleep in my room. I'll leave a note for my parents so when they get up in the morning, they'll know you're with me and that everything's cool."

"Listen, I don't want to get you in trouble. I mean, my mom might call here or something. I can stay in the garage and leave before anyone gets up. No one will even know I was here."

"You'll come inside. My parents love you and I love you. They know I'm a lesbian and one more queer in our house isn't going to faze them. C'mon, I'm freezing to death out here."

That night in Kay's bedroom she and Alex made love for the first and only time. She remembered every breath and touch like it was yesterday—the feel of Al's soft skin beneath her and the heady, dizzy feeling of kissing her for the first time. In the dim light of her bedroom, she softly kissed Alex's fresh bruises hoping to magically heal the pain.

"I love you, Kay. I'll always love you. Someday, you won't have to take care of me. I'll take care of you."

"Shhh. Let me make love to you again."

The feel of Alex's skin against her own reminded her of warm summer grasses in the field near her house. Al's kisses were the July sun, making Kay's face flush with desire. Alex twirled her fingers through Kay's hair and held her close as Kay's tongue darted across dark, hard nipples. The sighs Kay heard were like the wind across that same nearby field and she thought at that moment how wonderful it would be to make love to Alex in that field near the rushing stream when summer finally came.

Al never did go back home. She went to live with her aunt. A few years later, Al's mother was killed in a car accident. She drove drunk into a logging truck about a mile from their house and died instantly.

Twenty-five years later, they were walking arm in arm, Al's head leaning on Kay's shoulder at the shores of Cook Inlet. They never spoke of that night—of the passion that had gripped them in Kay's bedroom, the sound of the rain mixing with the moans of their pleasure. But Kay knew Al's memories were as intact as her own. She had read the memories in Al's eyes many times when a quick glance or smile said so much more than words. There was really no need to talk about it. What they needed and wanted to say had been said completely on that night those many years ago.

Kay squeezed Alex's hand, then turned to find Lela. She was walking a few paces behind them, hands shoved deep into her pockets, dark hair whipping in the wind, gray eyes scanning a shoreline that was still golden in the late evening sun. Feelings of guilt nagged at Kay as she continued walking hand in hand with Alex. She hoped that Lela still understood her need to concentrate on Alex during these past six months. Lela was a deeply spiritual woman who had the ability to connect with people through some inexplicable sixth sense. She responded immediately to the pain Kay felt after hearing the news of Alex's illness and had been more than understanding when Kay announced her decision to travel to Fairbanks, collect Alex, and bring her to live with them in Anchorage. There was a quiet strength about Lela that Kay greatly admired. But there were times when Kay was unable to gauge her partner's thoughts. During their last two years together, Kay had learned that Lela was a woman of few words. She let her actions do most of the talking, and her passion for Kay and the people she loved came across in creating a welcoming home, planning social occasions, and working long hours for the environmental causes important to Alaska's native people. Previous experiences with partners made Lela's complexities even more baffling. Barb, Kay's first partner, was vocal, verbally abusive, and completely domineering. Stef was emotional—even childlike. Stef used her femininity to her advantage, flirting to get her way and exerting her control of the relationship in the bedroom. Kay's relationship with Lela was a loving and nurturing conundrum that kept her constantly guessing.

"I remember a promise of ice cream," Lela said, putting her arms around both Kay and Alex from behind. "Is it time now?"

"It's time," Alex agreed. "Kay's treat, I'm thinking."

"You two take complete advantage of my good nature," Kay said while digging into her pocket for money. "But I guess some ice cream won't bankrupt me."

"Now you have two women in your home so you must be equal in the spoiling," Lela said with a grin. "It is a challenging task."

Alex put her arm through Lela's. "Lela, do you think Kay can handle the demands of two women in her life? That's a tall order."

"I think Kay must answer that question."

"There's no hope for me. I'm completely outclassed," Kay said with resignation. "It's tough living with two gorgeous women, but I guess I'll just have to suffer."

Wednesday arrived and Kay found herself once again in Russ's truck on their way to Denali to begin the investigation of the mining site near Sugarloaf. The tension between Russ and Kay was still palpable. They spoke sporadically over the last couple of days and only about business. There was no joking or lighthearted verbal sparring and the painful strain between them was beginning to wear on Kay. The last thing on earth she needed was a fracture in her friendship with Russ. For many years, he had been her rock and strongest supporter. She had come to rely on his strength and commonsense view of the world. And she couldn't imagine functioning at work on a daily basis without his knowledge and experience. But this rift between them was unlikely to heal anytime soon. There didn't appear to be any give on either side, especially with Kay's responsibility to ensure that there were no legal repercussions from the manager-subordinate relationship between Russ and Carla. Kay hated the timing of this rift, coming on the heels of Grace's visit and this trip to Sugarloaf. The whole situation had an uncomfortable foreboding.

"I sure hope this agent shows up at the appointed time and place," Kay said, struggling to start some kind of conversation.

Russ kept his eyes on the road. "You never know with this kinda stuff. I don't like the idea of workin' on somethin' this dangerous with someone we don't know. Hell, we don't even know his name."

"No, we don't. And I agree. In this situation, we don't have complete control and I guess that's freaking me out. We always have everything planned down to the last detail. But we're at the mercy of someone else now."

"Amen. This ain't the first time Grace Perry has gotten us into a mess and I'm guessin' it ain't the last."

"I just can't imagine that yellowcake is coming from Sugarloaf, Russ. So close to Denali. It just will not register in my brain. I can't come to grips with the possibility at all."

Russ glanced at Kay. His face was deeply marked with lines of stress, his features drawn and tired. "Listen, considerin' this information came from a bunch of senators and Grace Perry, I don't give it much credence. Not yet anyway."

An hour later, the main entrance to Denali was visible from the George Parks Highway. It was still early morning when Russ maneuvered the truck into the park entrance, the vehicle jostling roughly along the uneven gravel road to the park's central ranger station. Inside the large wooden building, Kay and Russ found the station fully staffed. Two rangers worked the information desk, counseling several tourists on various routes to the park's camping sites. Another ranger was explaining a map of Denali to a vacationing family.

"Kay, Russ, what a great surprise." Tom Barnett, superintendent of Denali, greeted Kay and Russ enthusiastically. "It's great to see you both. Can I help you with anything?"

"Good to see you, Tom. Russ and I are starting our campsite inspection tour this afternoon," Kay explained. "Connie's working on next year's budget and we've got to give her some accurate estimates for upgrades. How's everything going?"

"Great. Great. Our visitation stats are way up, as I'm sure you know. I'll be by the office next week to file some updated reports." Tom had just completed twenty years of service in Denali, ten as superintendent. Hair graying at the temples, he appeared very distinguished in his park ranger uniform, always immaculately pressed. His stomach hung slightly over his trouser belt betraying his love for his wife's cooking, which he bragged about whenever Kay was around. "So far, it's been a terrific summer season, Kay. No serious accidents. We're at full staff now and that's helping us to handle the increased activity."

"Glad to hear the good news, Tom. Russ and I need to make some quick calls and then head to Riley Creek. We've got a lot of ground to cover in the next few weeks."

"Sounds like you do. Now listen, Kay. You've got to come to dinner soon so Vera can make you one of her homemade pies. You too, Russ."

"If you've got one stashed in the refrigerator, I wouldn't mind a slice right now," Russ said.

"Yesterday, there was some blueberry left. But I'm afraid the staff took care of it. Food doesn't last long around here."

Russ frowned. "We have the same problem in Anchorage. Someone lays out a dozen doughnuts and I barely get my hands on one."

Kay laughed. "Don't believe a word he says. And next time you stop by the office, we'll set up a time for dinner. Thanks for the invitation, Tom."

After grabbing a cup of coffee, Kay and Russ both made some phone calls from the main office. Wanting an update on what was happening in Anchorage, Kay called Tammy.

"All quiet on this front," Tammy said. "Anything going on where you are?"

"No. But the day's not over yet. Grace hasn't called?"

"She sent an e-mail this morning asking if you guys had left. I told her you had."

"Good. Say, did you get a chance to look at the present I left you?"

"This little black box thingy?"

"Yes. Sorry I didn't get a chance to explain it to you. Do you know how to use it?"

"I read your note and the instructions. You send e-mails on it, right? Seems easy enough."

"It's called a BlackBerry. And, yes, you're right. It's for e-mails."

"And you want me to wait to hear from you on this thing?"

"Yes. Check it every day. In case there's some kind of emergency."

"Okay. No problem, Kay. Are you expecting trouble on this trip?"

"Don't know. But I trust you. And you're my last line of defense if something happens. Are you following me?"

"You bet."

"Just keep in mind that everything's confidential."

"Hey, that much I know. No loose lips here in Anchorage. What about Ron though? He always walks around here like he's lord and master when you and Russ are gone at the same time."

Kay gripped the phone even tighter. She had forgotten about Ron. "Don't worry about Ron. And don't tell him anything. He's got a big mouth."

"Don't I know it. He's been poking around your office again. I found him in there this morning with his feet up on your desk reading some budget reports and getting ready to open your mail."

"Lock my office and swallow the key."

Tammy laughed. "Listen, I threw him out of there real quick and he's majorly peeved. I'm locking all of your mail in my desk now. But I'll take care of him. No worries."

"If you have any more problems with him, send me an e-mail on that BlackBerry and I'll take care of him."

"Will do."

At about three o'clock, Russ and Kay left the main ranger station at the Denali entrance, again emphasizing to the staff that they would be conducting site inspections for the next several weeks. It took them about fifteen minutes to reach Riley Creek and pick up the supplies they stashed in the storage shed last Saturday. After loading the supplies into Russ's truck, they left immediately and continued on to the Nenana River.

The Nenana River's origin was in the glacier-capped mountains of the Nenana Mountain range. After making its way west from the frigid mountain heights between two massive glaciers, the river flowed into a lush green valley and then began a journey that paralleled the Denali Highway for about fifteen miles. Flat and calm, this stretch of river bed was perfect for kayaking. Further south near Panorama Mountain, the river was a whitewater rafting paradise with holes and waves that were both exhilarating and dangerous.

Russ and Kay camped out of sight in a grove of black spruce trees just off of the Denali Highway. The tall, lean spruce trees with small dark cones reminded Kay of giant pipe cleaners. Through the veil of head nets worn to protect them from hordes of mosquitoes, they watched golden eagles swoop down from the mountains, gliding on wind currents into the valley. At dusk, late into the evening, they watched deer and moose drink from the cool river water. When darkness fell completely, it was just before midnight. Under the cover of that darkness, they put into water and headed north to the mountains. By that time, the Alaskan Railroad had made its final trip through the valley, hauling tourists to Denali.

The kayakers they had seen all day were gone and the waterway was quiet and still. The two-person kayak cut through the water silently. The air was crisp and cool and the shoreline hummed with mosquitoes and other insects, the sound of snowshoe hares rustling in the brush, and lynx and red fox giving chase to that same prey. They stowed their gear in the storage compartments fore and aft, but each still carried a backpack, making paddling more tiresome. They were both covered with mosquito repellant but swatted them endlessly while struggling to paddle. Regardless, they made good time. Occasionally, they maneuvered close to the eastern shore to avoid dry sand beds. It had been an unusually hot summer in Denali and the river was low. A few times the kayak scraped bottom because of the heavy load, but they were never forced to leave the river, even though they had considered the possibility.

Three hours into their trip, Russ and Kay finally reached the northernmost edge of the valley. The banks became rockier and the wind swirled and whipped at the base of the mountains that led to Sugarloaf. The ground was covered with low shrubs that were able to survive cold temperatures. Blueberry, lowbush cranberry, crowberry, and labrador tea thrived and added color to an otherwise bleak landscape. Soon it would be light again so they worked quickly to unload and store the kayak in some underbrush east of the river. They repacked their gear and ended up with their original backpacks and one base camp duffel bag apiece. The first few miles were going to be hell—but once they formed their base camp, much of the gear would remain in camp. Russ and Kay looked up almost in unison. The rocky banks of Nenana were cut steeply from the water's edge. From here on in, they would be climbing up from the river valley and *taiga*, the Russian word for forested areas. As they ascended 1,700 feet, they would travel through the tundra and navigate the rock, grass, scrub, thicket, and boggy areas until they reached the base of Sugarloaf about three miles northeast.

"Shit," Russ said, squinting into the predawn shadows. "I'm gettin' too old for this."

Kay laughed to hide her own dread. "We may be advancing in years, Russ, but we haven't gotten soft behind those desks yet. Before we start climbing, I'm going to get some water samples so they can be tested for radiation levels."

"This is near where the Inuit fisherman got sick," Russ said, helping Kay with her equipment. "If this area of the river is contaminated, there's probably some funny-lookin' fish swimmin' under that water."

Kay began to fill some of the plastic tubes. "The thought of this river being contaminated makes me sick. It's Denali's eastern border and while Sugarloaf is beyond our jurisdiction, this river is not."

As they began their ascent from the valley floor, Kay thought about all of the hours she and Russ put into running and strength training. Russ was an imposing man, with broad shoulders and a barrel chest. But it was all muscle. Many nights they went straight from work to the gym where they ran the treadmills and lifted weights, spotting for one another. For a good portion of their workout, they concentrated on leg strength. They could both vigorously work the StairMaster for an hour at a time. As they strained up the hillside, Kay forced her mind to think of the hill as that StairMaster. Too bad she was carrying a twenty-pound bag of supplies and a twenty-pound backpack.

An hour into the hike, as the sun came up above the mountains in front of them, Kay was in a zone. That's where she put herself whenever she was faced with what seemed like an impossible challenge. She latched onto a memory and stayed with it, reliving it as though she was traveling back into another dimension of time and space.

It was Lela's voice she heard—faint but unmistakable—singing a song in the Inuit tongue that she had sung for Kay before. The meaning had been explained to her and she remembered it well. It was a song to the mountain spirits asking for an early spring and bountiful hunting grounds. The hunter kneeled and sang facing the great mountains in the north as he prepared for the next day's hunt. Kay's head rested on Lela's shoulder and she could feel the vibration of the song in Lela's lungs. The fire from the living room hearth crackled, the heat of the coals flushing Kay's face. The gentleness of Lela's fingers in her hair and the intonation of that song held her safe. There was a strength in Lela's gentleness that seemed to defy logic. Somewhere behind those misty gray eyes an old soul lived as though a thousand ages flowed through her veins and into Kay's heart. No anger lived there. Perhaps regret for the struggles of her people and the continual assault on the land that defined their very existence. Oh, there was resolve—strong and constant—a survival instinct that was never to be confused with weakness. It was the anger missing from the mix that Kay did not understand. The Inuit people were not an angry people. The absence of this anger confused Kay because the anger seemed justified and because she herself seemed to live with anger every day. It was Lela who diffused that anger, forcing her to make peace with it against her will.

"Thanks for the song. It always has a calming effect."

"You feel at peace now."

"Yes. Not a feeling I have very often. My mother always said I was a restless soul."

Lela kissed Kay's forehead. "So you are not content with peace."

"Not for long. I don't know why."

"It is your anger that makes you restless. Anger is not always bad, though it can be a poison."

"It hasn't poisoned you."

"*I have met it on my doorstep. That is what my husband believed. Meet anger on the doorstep and do not let it pass to take root in your house or heart. So far, I have been lucky. It has not entered.*"

"*I let it in. So many times. With my family, work, relationships. But not with you.*"

"*You have had some trying relationships.*"

"*That's true. I was never really angry with Stef. She was young and I knew better. But Barbara was another story. Controlling and smothering. Abusive. That made me angry—mostly because I didn't understand her anger.*"

"*That is in the past. You learned from it.*"

"*Then why am I still angry?*"

"*Maybe you are confusing anger with passion. I think you are very passionate about many things. Your work, your friends, your home.*"

"*You. I'm passionate about you.*"

Lela smiled and wrapped her arms around Kay's shoulders. "*That is a passion we share. The spirits have ordained it for us.*"

"*Which spirits are these? Not the same mountain spirits?*"

"*No, the mountain spirits guide us in the hunt. The fire spirits guide us in matters of the heart.*"

"*Then we shouldn't let this beautiful fire go to waste.*"

"*No. That would make the spirits angry.*"

Russ suddenly stopped about three feet in front of her. "Kay, let's knock off for an hour or so. We've got another hour to go but we're well ahead of schedule and we need to eat somethin'."

Kay could feel the sweat pouring down her back. Her right hand was numb from carrying the duffel bag. Her calves burned and her mouth was dry. The first thing she did was drain half of her water bottle. Then she sank to the ground, leaning her back against a huge boulder. Looking down over the valley, she was amazed at how far they had come. The Nenana River looked like a trickling stream from two miles up and the Denali Highway was nothing more than a trail line.

Glancing at Russ, Kay could see that he was tired. She shared that feeling but neither one would ever admit it. They had kept a brisk pace and were definitely ahead of schedule, as Russ said. Winded as they were, their fitness would have them back up and moving within the hour.

"What's for lunch?" Kay asked, watching Russ rummage through his backpack.

"I'm thinking some Slim Jims and trail mix."

"I'd eat the alder I'm so hungry. I haven't had anything to eat since early this morning."

"We'll fix ya up." Russ tossed Kay a package of Slim Jims. He opened the trail mix bag with his pocket knife and signaled for Kay to cup her hands. "This ought to get us movin' again."

The raisins, sunflower seeds, banana slices, and apricot chunks tasted like dinner at a four-star restaurant. The Slim Jim was strictly for energy and protein and had never been one of Kay's favorites.

"I wish we had a specific time for meeting our contact today," Kay said, taking another sip of water. "The vagueness of this rendezvous makes me uneasy."

"I figure we get to where we're supposed to be, set up base camp, and if no one shows up we investigate the mining camp on our own. To hell with Grace and her half-baked schemes." Russ unlaced his boots and rubbed his feet. "We've got to watch our own backs, Kay. That's my two cents' worth."

"Regardless of what happens, I'll watch your back and you watch mine."

"That's a given."

"So is small talk the new thing for us?"

Russ continued rubbing his feet. "Seems safer, don't it?"

"But it's not us. We've always been able to talk about things.

I've been thinking a lot about you and Jen. I know things can happen in relationships. It isn't always easy for Lela and me either."

"Hearin' you say that surprises me."

"I guess you never truly know a person. Not even good friends. I'm sorry I was so judgmental. Just don't want anything bad to happen to you. A lawsuit, an EEOC complaint would be devastating. You'd lose your job."

"It won't come to that. Carla's gonna quit her job. She's givin' her notice next week."

"And you and Jen?"

"Don't know yet. I've got a lot of thinkin' to do. What about you and Lela? You never said nothin' about bein' unhappy."

"It's not that I'm unhappy or that I don't love Lela, Russ, and maybe it's the same with you and Jen. Sometimes we just don't connect and that may be my fault, I don't know. Lela would say differently. To her, our relationship is very spiritual. That's part of her culture. And that's fine for her. But I'm more grounded. Things are pretty black and white with me. Life is what it is, you know?"

"Yeah. I follow ya. It's the day-to-day stuff. You get wrapped up in keepin' things together. Routine sort of stuff like payin' bills and keepin' the house up. Then there's two jobs and all. That's what a relationship becomes. There's somethin' good about it. Goin' down that road together and makin' it when times are tough. But then things happen. It can sometimes fall apart."

"Things happen all right. Friends get cancer."

"Is Lela cool about Alex livin' there?"

"Oh, yeah. She wouldn't have it any other way. But it's still stressful. The worry sucks the life out of you. Then Lela travels back and forth to Juneau and I get caught up in bizarre assignments like this." Kay adjusted the straps on her backpack. "Lela seems to casually accept these things while I feel like we're barely hanging on to each other."

When they finally reached their destination—the rendezvous point Grace had given them—Kay and Russ chose a base camp behind a rocky outcrop on a clump of grass. There were two small white spruces at their backs and the gray rock face in front of them. Kay looked up and guessed they were approximately three miles from the summit of Sugarloaf and another five miles from the mining camp located in the valley east of the summit. Russ began by setting up the main tent while Kay surveyed the grounds surrounding the camp. There were no tracks, no debris or garbage, no signs of anyone having been in the area recently. She did find a trickling waterfall that ran down the western face of the mountain and would provide an excellent water supply.

"No one's here but us. As near as I can figure out, nobody's been here recently," Kay reported to Russ.

"No sign of our friend, heh?"

"None."

Russ looked around warily. "Who knows. Maybe we're bein' watched right now."

"Maybe. All we can do is wait, I guess. One thing's for sure, we're done for the day. Let's finish setting up camp and then have something to eat."

"Don't have to ask me twice."

Inside the tent after dinner, Kay lay on her back wondering what the next day would bring. It was ten o'clock and she was exhausted. Russ snored loudly on the other side of the tent, his back toward her. In the middle of the tent a small gas lamp provided soft light and deep shadows. Kay thought about Alex and wondered how she was doing. Tomorrow she would BlackBerry a message to Tammy and have her contact Lela, letting Lela know that she and Russ were okay. She'd also have Tammy ask for an update on Alex. Along with fatigue, the shadows of the enclosed tent finally overcame Kay and she drifted into a sound sleep. She knew it was a sound sleep because her next memory was startling. She was having a dream that she couldn't breathe—a dream where the shadows smothered her, and she couldn't cry out. Her eyes opened to complete darkness. The gas lamp was out. And then she realized that there was a hand over her mouth and a gun at her head. She felt the cold metal of the barrel against her right temple and smelled the sweat of the person holding the gun—the person whose breath whispered coldly in the darkness.

"I'm going to remove my hand from your mouth. But the gun stays where it is. Call and wake your friend up, nice-like. Understand?"

Kay nodded, though still somewhat confused. It sounded like a woman's voice. But the voice had an edge to it and Kay did as instructed. The hand slid from her mouth and Kay cleared her throat. For a brief moment, no words came. Her heart was beating hard and her face was hot with fear. "Russ," she croaked. "Russ, wake up."

A grunt came from Russ's direction. "What the hell?"

"Wake up, Russ," Kay said again in a stronger voice.

Kay heard Russ move and caught a beam of light out of the corner of her eye. Russ must have turned on a flashlight.

"Hey, what the hell's goin' on?"

"Take it easy big guy. No sudden moves," the strange voice warned. "You Russell Bend?"

"Yeah. Who the hell are you?"

"This Kay Westmore?"

Russ's voice grew more assured. "Yeah, that's Kay Westmore. I'm askin' ya one last time. Who the hell are you?"

"Tory Mitchell, Central Intelligence Agency."

"I'm real impressed. Now take that gun away from Kay's head," Russ demanded.

"Sure thing, big guy. Sorry about that, miss." Tory Mitchell removed the gun from Kay's temple and Kay sat up, turning around to face the agent. "Identification," the agent barked.

Kay and Russ, making no sudden movements, dug out their government credentials. The agent inspected each card closely with a mini flashlight. "These appear to be in order."

Kay slid the ID card back into her wallet. "Was the gun absolutely necessary?" Kay asked angrily, still groggy and confused.

"Pays to be careful," Tory replied. "One can't be sure who anyone is."

Russ relit the gas lamp. "You got one helluva nerve, lady. I don't care who the hell you are. There was no need to sneak in here and play secret agent. Who else would be in this tent waiting all night for your ass to show up?"

"Don't know, Mr. Bend. But that's the kind of job I have—one where you can never be sure who anyone is."

"Even if that's true," Kay offered in a conciliatory tone, "there was no need to put a gun to my head. I don't appreciate your methods of surprise even if you feel they were necessary. Russ and I work for the government, too. You saw our credentials. All you had to do was wake us up and check them."

"That sounds polite, Ms. Westmore. But it's not the world I live in."

There was an accent to the agent's voice that Kay couldn't identify. Maine? New Hampshire? Her words came in a staccato—quick and to the point. "Well, can we get some more sleep or do we need to have further conversation at this very moment?"

"I'm already back in the sack," Russ growled, extinguishing the lamp and turning away from them.

"He always so grumpy?" Tory asked.

"I think he has a right to be. You have your own tent?"

"Don't need one. Thanks."

Within moments, the agent was gone. Despite an uneasiness Kay couldn't shake, she finally fell into a restless sleep.

Light seeping into the tent suddenly woke Kay. She looked at her watch and noted that it was just past five o'clock. It had been light for at least an hour, but the previous day's hike had caused Kay to sleep longer than usual. She was always an early riser and would normally have gotten up at first light. Russ was still sleeping so Kay moved quietly from the tent out into the chilly July morning. She quickly surveyed the surrounding area and saw no sign of Tory Mitchell. Was their frightening encounter earlier that morning a dream? For a brief moment she wondered until she heard Tory say, "Morning, Ms. Westmore. Sleep okay?"

"No thanks to you, but yes," Kay said crisply.

"We got off on the wrong foot, but once your partner gets up, I'll brief both of you. Maybe you'll understand why caution is necessary. Not that I care," Tory added quickly. "My job's not about winning popularity contests."

Kay crawled back into the tent and grabbed one of the base camp duffels that contained food, coffee, and other supplies. She dragged it from the tent and set up a small stove near the rock face. While she made some coffee, she studied Tory Mitchell from a distance. Crouched on the ground just outside the tent, Tory smoked a cigarette. She was younger than Kay—in her mid-thirties, Kay guessed. About five-foot-nine, the agent was lanky and very trim, obviously conditioned due to the nature of her work. It surprised Kay that Tory smoked, but she still appeared very fit. She had short auburn hair with blond highlights and forest green eyes—an unusual deep green color that caught Kay's attention immediately. She wondered if Tory wore those special contacts lenses that changed the color. Dressed in olive cargo pants and a black, long-sleeved wind shirt, Tory looked like any other Denali tourist, except for the bulge underneath her wind shirt that Kay knew was a gun.

"Coffee?" Kay offered in a more pleasant tone.

Tory reached for the steaming cup. "Thanks."

"I've got some trail mix and can make some oatmeal, if you'd like."

"Sounds good."

"Feedin' the enemy?" Russ asked, emerging from the tent. He stopped and stretched, scratching his stomach through a buttoned camouflage shirt that had seen considerable wear and should have been trashed long ago. "Ain't this cozy."

"Morning, Mr. Bend," Tory said in between sips of coffee. "You going to hold our encounter this morning against me?"

"Listen, I don't mind havin' my sleep disturbed. But I do mind seein' a gun pointed at my boss's head."

Kay interrupted. "Russ, have some coffee and something to eat. Let's hear what Agent Mitchell has to say."

Russ glared at Tory and then abruptly turned away. He and Kay grabbed some coffee and oatmeal and sat down on the ground facing Tory who warmed her hands with the tin of coffee.

"So enlighten us," Russ said sarcastically. "I'm all ears."

Tory lowered the coffee mug and flashed those green eyes, which seemed to drill right through Kay. "First, let's ditch the formalities. Call me Tory. Agent Mitchell isn't necessary. I'll call you by your first names. Make things easier. Agreed?"

"Suits me," Russ said. "I hate bein' called Mr. Bend. Reminds me of Grace Perry. That I can do without."

Kay looked at Tory and shrugged. "Kay's fine. Whatever."

"Good. Now we get down to business." Tory took another sip of coffee. She held the cup in Kay's direction. "Good coffee."

"Thanks."

"I'm guessing that Grace Perry gave you the lowdown as to why we're here."

"In her own charming style," Kay answered.

"No doubt." Tory pulled a map out of her backpack. She sat Indian style with the map resting on her lap, oriented to face Kay and Russ. "Then you know about the mining camp in the valley just east of Sugarloaf. And about the uranium ore that we suspect is coming out of there. But how it's being mined, transported out of that valley, and refined into yellowcake is what we don't know. We do know it's making its way to the Middle East. That fact is disturbing to the United States government, as you can imagine. We've actually pinpointed the sale of some yellowcake in Cairo. We're assuming it's the same stuff."

"Egypt?" Kay asked with surprise. "Grace mentioned Africa. That the shipments were going to Africa and then to the Middle East."

"That's what we originally thought. But it's gotten scarier since then. Egypt is supposed to be one of our diplomatic *friends*," Tory said with sarcasm. "But Egypt is a dangerous friend. The kind of friend who offers to light your cigarette with one hand while planting a dagger in your belly with the other. Where the yellowcake is going once it leaves Cairo and whether or not the Egyptian government knows about it or is involved, is unsubstantiated."

"So we're gonna go pokin' around that mining camp to see if we can figure out how they're transportin' the ore. Is that the idea?"

Tory nodded. "That's right. If the ore is coming from that mine, we're going to follow it and see where it leads us. We've already lost two CIA agents in Cairo who were on the trail from that end."

"What do you mean when you say *lost*?" Kay asked.

"Assassinated. They were getting close to the source at their end. We were working backwards from Cairo to the source of the ore. Trying to put a stop to the shipments by identifying those receiving the ore in Cairo and shipping it to wherever from there." Tory ran her fingers through her hair and slowly exhaled a cloud of cigarette smoke. "Since losing two agents, we've changed our tactics. We're tappin' you guys to help us since you're outside of the usual government intelligence community. We're afraid there's an informant on the inside tipping our hand and exposing our agents."

"What about you?" Kay asked. "You're on the inside of the intelligence network. Isn't that a bit dangerous for you? For us?"

"I'm what they call a *rogue*," Tory explained. "Nobody knows about me."

Russ shook his head. "How's that possible?"

"It's possible. That's all I can say. You're the only two people on the face of the earth who know about me. Not even Grace Perry knows who I am. Not the Senate, the CIA director, the FBI, the NSA. No one. On paper, I don't exist."

Russ looked at Kay and Kay met his stare. For one of the few times since she'd known Russ, she detected panic in his eyes.

"You guys look like you ate bad food."

"How would you expect us to look after a briefing like this?" Kay asked, trying to suppress the fear in her voice.

"Like you ate bad food. But I need you. You know this terrain, this area, and the indigenous people here. All of that is key. Don't have to tell you how important this job is. The mess our government's in speaks for itself. We live in a new world where the purveyors of terror wear many faces and operate from many locations. Even from the beauty of Alaska."

"That's hard to deny," Kay agreed. "But let's get one thing straight. Russ and I aren't going to prance around the Sugarloaf Valley dressed in our ranger uniforms pretending to take water samples. You were to be a staffer from the EPA assisting us with our work. That's what Grace suggested as a cover."

"Jesus," Tory said in disbelief. "We can't be doing that shit. We need to move around undetected."

"My point exactly. This area's well beyond our Denali jurisdiction. Our cover wouldn't hold up for two seconds. Not to mention the fact that the mining company's private property."

"Kay, not to worry. We're on the same page. Where I need your help is the best route down into the valley."

"Russ and I mapped one out using topographical maps of the area." Kay unfolded the map illustrating the highlighted route.

"This route skirts two small Inuit villages and also takes us north of the camp used by mining company employees."

Tory studied the map intently. "Excellent work. This is perfect. The area you've chosen as a forward base camp will give us an excellent vantage point of the mining operation."

About an hour later, after they repacked their gear, Tory took Kay aside. She stood toe to toe with Kay, hands on hips. Kay felt like her personal space was being invaded. "Listen, when we get to the forward base camp you've identified near the mining camp, I want Russell to stay behind and stand guard. As you made very clear, all of our movements need to be undetected. My military training says always have someone watching your rear." Tory ran her fingers through her short, wiry hair, a nervous habit Kay had already observed. "So I need Russ to stay behind while we go into the camp after dark. Think he's going to be a pain in the ass about this?"

"It won't make him happy, but Russ will do what he's asked. He may seem uncooperative, but it's more wariness than anything else. We've been through a lot together."

"Understood. I sense that Russell is the guy—maybe the only guy—we'd want watching out for us."

"In my opinion, that's correct."

"Hey, what's that?" Tory asked, eyeing Kay's BlackBerry.

"It's the messenger Grace gave me to keep in touch. I'm supposed to send a message every day at five o'clock sharp. I was just fiddling with it to see if it worked."

"Oh, really? Russell got one, too?"

"Yes."

Tory called for Russ and he appeared from behind a tree. "Sorry to disturb you but can I see your BlackBerry?" Tory held out her hand.

"Yeah, no problem. I wasn't plannin' on usin' the blasted thing anyway." Russ tossed the small black box in Tory's direction.

"Kay, yours please."

Kay handed Tory the BlackBerry. "Problem?"

"Hell, yes there's a problem!" Kay listened in stunned silence as Tory unleashed a stream of obscenities directed at the United States government, the Senate, and Grace Perry. "Stupid, stupid people. It's one thing to act on important intelligence information to protect the citizens of this country. But then you need to butt out!" Tory threw the BlackBerrys onto the ground and stomped on both with the heel of her boot. Several loud crunches later, shattered pieces littered the ground. Tory scooped them up and flung them over the rock face where they floated out of sight onto the tundra below.

"Geez, I think they at least deserved a proper burial," Russ said solemnly, craning his neck over the rock face.

"What is wrong with you?" Kay asked, dumbfounded.

"Great way to let the entire fucking world know where we are. I supposed Perry had a temporary transmission tower erected around here, too," Tory said while pacing back and forth.

"I'd say that's a pretty good guess," Russ said.

"Damn her! Do you guys get how dangerous that is?"

"Actually, Kay tried to persuade Grace that the things wouldn't work," Russ offered.

"It's a traceable signal. Understand?"

"Of course," Kay answered. "But the problem no longer exists, does it?"

"Thankfully, no. Now, maybe we can get through this mission without getting killed." Tory kicked at the dirt, fingers darting through her hair.

"I'm all for that," Kay agreed. "What I don't care for is your attitude. If the BlackBerrys needed to be disposed of, you could have told us in a civilized manner. Is it necessary to be such a brute about everything?"

Tory started to laugh. "Brute? You think I'm a brute?" With a grin and a leering glance, Tory said, "Hell, I'll consider that a compliment, Kay. Try to keep in mind, however, that agents are being killed. I repeat, killed. If that calls for brutality on my part, then you won't get any apologies from me."

Just after noon on Thursday, they began their journey toward the summit of the mountain and the mining camp in the valley beyond. Although she didn't mention the BlackBerrys again, Kay could tell Tory was still seething about their existence. Tory walked with a resolve that sent a clear message of disgust. The climb to the peak of Sugarloaf was made easier by temperatures in the upper fifties and an overcast sky. Crisscrossing the terrain, the climbers moved across solid rock face and occasionally clumpy grass and dirt in between. It was not a steep climb but more gradual. Kay took the lead with a map and compass close at hand, but Tory was on her heels the entire way. Russ brought up the rear and was completely silent, an unusual occurrence. Occasionally, Tory lit a cigarette and despite this unhealthy habit, had no trouble keeping up with Kay who continued an aggressive pace. Kay could only shake her head in disbelief and keep moving, her own calf muscles burning after the two-hour trek over rugged ground.

Another hour brought them to the summit and a much needed rest. Kay brewed coffee and Russ made soup. Tory sat alone on a rocky outcrop, head buried in a map. She drank some water, chewed Slim Jims and smoked a few more cigarettes.

"What d'ya think of our agent friend?" Russ asked, pushing his sunglasses onto his forehead. "Ain't she a peach?"

"I haven't formed an opinion yet," Kay answered. "That stunt early this morning with the gun pissed me off, that's for sure. And the BlackBerry thing was over the top. But agents are being killed so I guess I can understand to some degree why she felt the need to introduce herself that way. And why she wouldn't want any communication going out or coming in."

"She's a loose cannon, if you ask me."

"Her methods are harsh. But she probably doesn't trust us any more than we trust her. And from her perspective, I can see why."

"Macho-agent-James-Bond-sneaking-around-in-the-middle-of-the-night crap, if you ask me. Yeah, folks are bein' killed—so she says. Everyone's been throwin' us bits of information, scraps of clues. If you ask me, we don't know shit. The only way we're gonna know anything is by waitin' and watchin'. It's like a giant puzzle and they're feedin' it to us piece by piece."

"You think Grace and Tory are misleading us?"

"Don't know. Hell, they don't even know each other accordin' to our friend over there. Accordin' to her, she don't exist. Ain't that somethin'? I wonder if she pays taxes."

Kay poured another cup of coffee. "I have to admit that the 'I don't exist' line sort of threw me. I mean, how is that possible? Someone must know she exists."

"Maybe she's a figment of her own imagination," Russ said with a smirk. "Personally, I don't like her."

"It's a little early to make judgments like that, isn't it?"

"You think I'm wrong?"

"We only met her twelve hours ago, Russ."

"Yeah, and we've known her twelve hours too long in my book."

"Well, we have to work with her. We don't have a choice. Besides, I'm still sizing her up. She seems pretty capable to me so far."

"Sizing her up?"

"The same thing you're doing, Russ. We're both doing it because so much depends on her decisions and judgments."

"Yeah. Like our lives. Maybe that's why I don't like her. The only people I trust with our lives is us."

Tory folded her map then dropped an unfinished cigarette, grinding it out with the heel of her boot. She approached the makeshift camp with her hands shoved into her pants pockets, map tucked under her arm. "Having a nice chat, I see. Mind if I have a cup of coffee?"

"Not at all." Kay poured the coffee and handed Tory the mug. "What's all the discussion about?"

Russ fiddled with his backpack, leaving Kay to answer. "We were just discussing the weather. We've been lucky so far. But I think our luck's about to run out. It's supposed to rain all day tomorrow. Going to be cold and miserable."

Tory grimaced. "That won't be fun. Listen, I figure we've got another three-hour trek into the valley. Then we wait until it gets dark before getting a closer look at the camp."

"What exactly will we be lookin' for?" Russ asked, suddenly joining the conversation.

"You need certain equipment and chemicals to refine uranium ore into yellowcake and once I spot any of that stuff, I'll need to record the evidence, get some samples and find out how it's being shipped. And where."

"And just what'll Kay and I be doin' while you're lookin' for this stuff? Sippin' a cup of Joe?"

"Watching out for my ass."

"Yes, ma'am," Russ said with a mock salute. "Whatever you say."

"That's right. Whatever I say. You have trouble taking orders from a woman?"

"My boss is a woman," Russ replied, nodding in Kay's direction. "We ain't never had a problem. I trust her."

"You don't trust me. Is that the inference?"

"I don't know you."

"I can say the same."

"I think you know a helluva lot more about me and Kay than we know about you."

"That may be true. But even if I didn't, my job is to get the information I need with your assistance. We didn't ask to be colleagues, but we are going to work together."

"I don't like bein' threatened in the middle of the night with a gun. And I don't like it that you don't exist. That's a mighty fine convenience if you want to suddenly disappear and leave us stranded here in the middle of some CIA mess. And without BlackBerrys or any other means of communicatin'."

"That's enough, Russ," Kay said, dumping the rest of her coffee on the ground. "I think it's time to move. Unless you disagree, of course," Kay said, deferring to Tory.

"No. You're absolutely right," Tory said with a distinct edge to her voice. "Enough's been said. In fact, too much. Time to go."

A few hours later, Kay stooped behind some rocks overlooking the valley and the mining camp to the east of Sugarloaf. Heavy equipment roared and echoed up the mountainside. The camp was busy with activity, crawling with mining personnel. It was a giant wound, a gouge in the valley floor, the mine that was supposed to be extracting platinum from the earth to create hydrogen-powered cars, a cleaner form of energy. Kay tried to imagine what the valley looked like before the government granted a lease to the mining company. She envisioned a lush green paradise resting peacefully, protected by the rocky peaks surrounding it. Inhabited by moose, bear, fox, wild sheep, and other wildlife, the valley had been crisscrossed by small streams running clean and clear across the valley floor and into the vast forests farther east. Whatever the valley had been, it was no more. But there were no signs of uranium mining—at least none that Kay noticed. She had studied pictures of uranium mines and the telltale sign was an evaporation pond of radioactive uranium tailings. This was, in effect, a sludge pond of unusable heavy metals and other contaminants, such as arsenic, left over during the milling process. Kay saw nothing in the valley below that indicated the mining of uranium. The large mountains of ore indicated a platinum mine. Tons of ore were processed to extract platinum and this mine certainly gave the appearance of being a legitimate platinum mining operation.

Tory moved into position next to her. "Busy place, heh?"

"Yeah. It certainly appears like your average platinum mining operation."

Tory agreed. "It does. I've looked at hundreds of pictures and there's nothing to suggest uranium mining here. That makes our job all the more interesting, don't you think?"

"No doubt. Where's Russ?"

"Setting up a temporary forward camp. He's very upset with me."

"Why? What did you say to him this time?"

"Nothing, except that I needed him to stay at camp tonight while you and I take a look at that." Tory pointed at the mine. "I don't think he likes the arrangement."

"I'll take care of it. Just don't antagonize him, okay? We've got enough to worry about."

"He's very protective of you."

"Like I told you before, we've worked together for a long time."

Tory rested her hand on Kay's shoulder. "Oh, listen. I understand. I'd be the same way."

Kay studied Tory's eyes. A sudden gentleness appeared and it startled her. To this point, the agent had been all business. "We should go back. I'll talk to Russ."

"Wait. I want to apologize," Tory said with a grimace. "Apologize for losing it about the BlackBerrys and for putting a gun to your head. But you've got to understand something." Tory's eyes glistened. "So far, I've lost two colleagues on this mission. One of them I didn't know as well. But he was a very competent, well-respected agent. Had a family. The other agent I knew very well. He and I went through training together. I loved him. I just don't want any more lives lost. Think you can understand that?"

"Of course. You're doing your job. And I'm very sorry about your colleagues. It's a tragedy that they've lost their lives. Don't mind Russ. He's a good guy—just a little hot under the collar. Like you, I'm afraid."

"Too much alike. That's never a good thing. But I sense that you're tough, too."

"I can be."

Early Friday morning, when it was finally dark, Kay and Tory knelt just outside the trailer that appeared to be the mining camp's main office. Russ reluctantly stayed behind after a bitter argument with Kay. Quickly, Kay buried the thought to keep her mind in the moment. She had been wrong about the rain. The sky was clear with a half-moon that cast too much light onto the valley floor.

Tory pointed to the trailer entrance and whispered, "Going inside. Watch my back. Anybody shows up, press this." Tory handed Kay a small square device with a button. "Depress the button and you'll see a red light. It'll send me a signal." Tory held up an identical unit.

Kay nodded. Through binoculars, they observed two security guards on the premises. Each was positioned at security shelters located at the north and south gates, which opened to admit trucks and other heavy equipment. Tory and Kay used wire cutters to cut through the fence along the western perimeter before making their way to the trailer.

Slithering up the steps to the trailer door, Tory deftly picked the lock and disappeared inside. Kay knelt in the shadows, away from the spotlight that illuminated the trailer. She concentrated on every sound and peered into the darkness for any movement nearby. It was eerily quiet, except for the ever-present whine of mosquitoes, which attacked her face and hands. The night was cool, causing Kay to dig into her jacket for gloves. The electronic signaling device Tory had given her hit the ground, bounced, and disappeared into the shadows. Kay cursed, shoved the gloves back into her jacket, and felt the ground around her, frantically searching for the tiny device. She didn't dare use her pocket flashlight, so she prayed and continued to claw at the ground, hoping for a miracle. The miracle happened when she bumped the device with her wrist, grabbed it, and closed her hand tightly around it. Her heart was thumping wildly. As Tory exited the trailer, crawling down the steps and into the shadows next to her, Kay exhaled slowly and silently thanked the spirits Lela claimed were everywhere.

Tory pointed to a stack of crates about twenty feet from the trailer, located well into the shadows. Crouching low to the ground, they moved toward the crates and stooped behind them.

"Find anything?" Kay asked anxiously.

"Safe beneath the floor," Tory whispered. "Took photos of maps. Looked like maps of the mine tunnels. Pages and pages of them. This place has tunnels that extend for miles underground. Some seem to extend far north of here, well beyond the working area of this mining operation. Find that interesting?"

"I certainly do. What now?"

"There's another trailer near the north gate. Want to check that one out, too."

"Is that necessary?" Kay argued. "This trailer is clearly the main office. The other one is probably used for storage. Why risk it?"

"We're here now. May not get another chance."

"Fine. Let's go," Kay whispered edgily.

Kay followed Tory's shadow as they zigzagged between tool and equipment sheds, stacks of crates, and the heavy machinery used to move the giant mounds of earth piled all around them. When they reached the second trailer, Tory again disappeared inside and Kay was left to decipher every sound. With no place to hide, she crouched at the rear of the trailer, frequently peering over each shoulder. There were lights outside the trailer entrance and she felt exposed. And then he was there, standing over her, as if he had been spawned by the night air itself into human form.

"Who the hell are you?"

Kay stood up and found herself staring at the barrel of a gun for the second time in two days. The middle-aged man was dressed in a security guard uniform and his glare was menacing. "I'm lost," she blurted without really thinking. "I'm a tourist, sir, and I'm lost. What is this place?"

"You're on private property," he snarled, edging closer. He had a thick accent and in the halo of light where he now stood, Kay noticed his skin tone was dark.

"I'm awfully sorry, sir," Kay said in the most demure voice she could muster. "I've been hiking and got lost yesterday. When I saw the lights down here, I thought maybe I could find someone to help me."

"Where's your backpack? Your hiking gear?" he asked suspiciously.

"Sir, I've been walking forever. I'm tired and hungry. I left the backpack up there." Kay pointed to the hills of Sugarloaf behind her. "Couldn't carry it anymore."

"I don't believe you."

"Listen, if you've got a phone or radio nearby, I can call the ranger station in Denali. I hear they pick you up if you're lost."

"You're not in Denali, lady."

"I'm not? You mean I'm so lost I wandered *outside* of the park? Shit, I'm really messed up."

Kay stared into the guard's dark eyes. He was busy processing everything she had said, trying to find the truth in her story, even though there wasn't any. The hand holding the gun moved, but Kay would never know if it moved to put the gun away or pull the trigger. In an instant, the body of the guard slumped to the ground and Tory stood in his place, a knife in her hand—its edge dripping blood.

Kay peered down at the guard. The wound across his neck pumped blood onto the ground. His eyes were wide open. "He's dead. Jesus, Tory, you killed him."

"He was about to kill you."

Kay looked up at Tory. Her face betrayed no emotion. "I'm not so sure. I think he was putting his gun away. That he was going to let me go."

"You're more naïve than I thought. He wasn't going to let you go. C'mon, we've got to drag him out of view and then get the hell out of here." Tory wiped the knife blade on her pants and slid it into its sheath. She grabbed the guard underneath the armpits and glared at Kay. "C'mon. Grab his legs!"

Taking hold of his boots, Kay helped Tory slide the body behind a stack of diesel barrels. Tory began to search his pockets, pulling out papers and identification.

"Is that necessary?"

"Yes. Going to have the CIA run a check on him. See what they come up with."

"Hurry. We need to get moving."

"You're right. His friend at the south gate is bound to call for a security check at some point. Probably on the hour." Tory checked her watch. "That gives us exactly eight minutes."

Russ was waiting for them at the temporary camp. Tory ordered him to pack all of the supplies and retreat to the permanent base camp on the west side of Sugarloaf's summit. They covered the distance quickly and silently. Every time Russ tried to find out what had happened, Tory ordered him to keep quiet. By the time they made base camp four hours later, tempers had flared to the boiling point.

"What the fuck is her problem?" Russ asked, as Tory disappeared inside the main tent.

Kay sat on the ground, head resting in her hands. "We got caught. Tory killed one of the guards."

"What? Are you fuckin' kiddin' me?" Russ asked in disbelief.

"Do I sound like I'm kidding?" Kay snarled. "It was awful. She slit his throat right in front of my eyes."

"Jesus Christ."

"She says he was about to shoot me. I don't know. Maybe he was. I just don't know."

Tory emerged from the tent with her backpack. "We've got to move. Back to Riley Creek. Got to get the pictures I took of the tunnel maps uploaded. We can't do anything without those maps."

"What maps?" Russ asked.

"Maps of the Sugarloaf Valley Mining Company," Kay answered. "There are miles and miles of tunnels running underground, crisscrossing the valley in every direction."

"The trailer was full of maps hidden in a safe underneath the floor," Tory said, tightening the straps of her backpack across her shoulders. "When we come back here, they're going to come in mighty handy."

Russ walked up to Tory and stood, arms crossed in front of him. "You're awfully calm for someone who just murdered a man."

"Was trained to kill people. Comes with the territory."

"That right? Well, it don't come with my territory. They're gonna find that guy and when we come back, they'll be waitin' for us."

"I agree that it will heighten their alert. We'll just have to be more careful," Tory said, turning away. "Now, are you two coming or not?"

Kay got up and brushed the dirt from her pants. "We're coming. Let's go, Russ."

Ten minutes later, under Kay's supervision, the camp was broken down. Nothing that indicated a camp was left behind. Kay then led the trio in a brisk retrace of their steps, returning down

79

the western face of Sugarloaf to the Nenana River. There would be no sleep, no rest breaks. When they reached Riley Creek, Kay told Tory that she would have use of the Interior Department's computer, which had a secure Internet connection. Tory's plan was to upload the mine photographs, send them to be analyzed, and have them converted into high-resolution files. The files would then be e-mailed to the only person Kay trusted—Tammy at the Anchorage office. Tammy would be instructed to print the documents and deliver them personally to Riley Creek.

To make matters more difficult, because they had only a two-man kayak available to navigate the Nenana River, they were forced to travel an additional ten miles on foot before they reached Russ's truck, which was located off-road about a half mile from the main entrance of Denali. This put Russ in an even more irritable mood, and he refused to speak to Kay or Tory as they drove the few miles back to Riley Creek.

Once at Riley Creek late Friday afternoon, Russ separated from Kay and Tory, seeking out the companionship of Carla, which irritated Kay but also ensured no further outbursts of temper between Tory and Russ. Kay had endured enough of that nonsense and needed some time to think. She also knew she faced the unpleasant task of contacting Grace Perry who had been expecting to hear from her on a daily basis. The BlackBerry smashing incident eliminated that option. Kay knew that Grace would be furious and could only imagine the tongue-lashing that was to come. But Kay's first phone call would not be to Grace.

Entering the ranger's office, Kay found Hugh Tucker sitting at the desk paging through some reports on the future upgrades proposed at Riley Creek. Hugh was near retirement and very soft-spoken. Sensing that Kay was in need of privacy, Hugh smiled and got up from the desk.

"You probably need to make some calls. I've got to unpack some tourist literature we got in today. Maps, brochures, and things."

"I see we've got a full campsite, Hugh."

"Oh, yes ma'am. We've had a full campsite all summer. And I expect it will only get better once the upgrades are done next year. I'm amazed that the government's going to allocate those funds."

"They really have no choice. Things are getting pretty bad, as you know, and Denali is one of the most popular vacation destinations in the country. Something has to be done."

"Obviously good news for us. See you later."

"Thanks, Hugh." Kay pushed aside the reports that were strewn across the desk and slumped down into the swivel chair. She put her head in her hands and felt exhaustion seeping into her bones. But there was still so much to do. The first call she made was to Lela. Alex answered the phone.

"Al, how are you?"

"Kay, we've been thinking about you. How's the trip going?"

"Everything's cool. How you feeling?"

"Pretty good."

"You sound great."

"Lela's been taking terrific care of me. She's in Seward right now but only for the day. Meeting with one of the Inuit environmental councils. She'll be back late tonight. I know she's anxious to talk to you. Will you call back?"

"Tell her that I'll call tomorrow. I'm really beat."

"I'll give her the message. You do sound tired. Are you sure you're okay?"

"Fine, fine. Russ and I covered a lot of ground yesterday. The sooner this job is done, the sooner I'll get back to my two favorite women. I miss you both."

"We miss you, too. We're planning a big celebration when you get back, okay?"

"Can hardly wait. Call me at Riley Creek if you need me. I'll be here for the next twenty-four hours at least. In the meantime, you take care. Rest, hear me?"

"Will do. Love you."

"Love you, too."

Kay felt a great sense of relief as she hung up the phone. Just hearing Al's voice was a comfort. The next numbers she punched were to the office. Tammy answered on cue.

"I've been worried sick about you and Russ," Tammy said, clearly flustered. "No e-mails on this berry thingy. Nothing at all. What happened?"

"We're fine. You can ditch the BlackBerry. Long story. Listen, I really need your help." Kay explained about the e-mail Tammy would receive in a couple of hours. "I need you to print the files and deliver them personally, okay? And don't say a word about this to Ron."

"Are you kidding? I've been keeping my eye on him. I've had to lock up everything in sight with all his poking around. So don't worry about me saying boo to him about this."

"Great. Thanks."

"What's the agent like?"

"Agent?"

"The CIA agent you were supposed to meet," Tammy said with exasperation. "Did he show up or what?"

"*She* showed up and that's a story I'll save for when I get back."

"She? Cool! That must have been a surprise."

"Kinda. Yeah."

"Listen, Grace Perry has been calling me every day. Man, she is peeved. You better call her, Kay. She's been threatening to fly to Anchorage, hire some bloodhounds, and track you down personally. I stare at the front door all day waiting for her to bust in with half the Senate and the rest of Congress in tow."

Kay laughed and heard Tammy laughing at the other end. "Sorry you've been on the receiving end of Grace's wrath. That's my next call, and I'm not looking forward to it."

"Guess I'll be seeing you tomorrow afternoon. You sound tired. Hang in there, boss."

"Thanks. See you tomorrow."

Kay hung up the phone and paused before hitting the numbers to Grace's office from the sheer intimidation of it. Somehow, she found the strength and after being transfered several times finally heard Grace's curt hello. Kay got about three words out of her mouth before the verbal barrage began.

"How dare you ignore my orders. They were utterly clear. Contact me every day with an update. Your actions are inexcusable . . ." and on and on. Finally, there was a pause in the verbal onslaught and Kay managed to blurt, "Grace, I followed the instructions given by the agent assigned to this mission. I had no choice."

"Who is this agent? Put him on the phone. I'll make sure he understands who's in charge here."

"He's a *she*, and she's busy right now." Kay gave Grace a complete blow-by-blow update about the smashed BlackBerrys, what had been found at the camp, the killing of the security guard, and the need to return to Riley Creek. There was silence on the other end.

"I don't like the sound of this. I'm pulling you out of there, Kay. Russ, too. I don't want you in those tunnels. God knows what's under there. And the killing of the guard is going to make it all the more difficult to get back in there. No, it's too dangerous."

"The danger will be greater for all of us, Grace, if there is uranium being mined from this area and yellowcake continues to make its way to Egypt and then God knows where from there. Can we really afford to divert our attention from this mission?"

There was an audible sigh and then, "No. But I feel responsible for your safety. I must be getting too old for this crap because I care. I never used to care. But I do care now. Very much."

Kay was touched. Finally, there had been a crack in the tough façade of Grace Perry. "I think we've got to see this one through to the end."

"Fine. Listen to this agent. Follow her instructions. Contact me when you can but only when it's safe to do so."

"Will do, Grace."

"One last thing, Kay. Keep your eyes open. Follow your instincts. This entire matter is growing more complex by the day. It's hard to know whom to trust. I'm appalled to say that I don't even trust the people I'm working for."

"That's not good news."

"Oh, you know how I am. I've become an expert at flushing out the Washington wolves. Or at least diverting their attention to other prey. But I don't want to talk in riddles. Just be careful."

Hanging up the phone, Kay paused for a moment trying to absorb what Grace had said. She talked in riddles, which concerned Kay even more. But deciphering the riddles would have to wait because she could barely keep her eyes open.

"Hey, you okay?" Tory asked, peeking inside the door.

"Yeah, fine."

"Tammy okay with the delivery?"

"No problem."

"Can I come in?"

"Sure."

"You talk with Perry?"

"Yeah. Just finished the call."

"She give you a hard time?"

"At first."

Tory sat on the edge of the desk. "Perry's smart from what you've told me and from what I've heard. It's one thing to be in Washington making decisions about investigations like these. Filtering through intelligence reports and acting on the crucial ones. But then you've got to pass the ball on to field agents and that means passing control—understanding that certain decisions need to be made based on the here and now. And they have to be made apart from static reports and week- or month-old intelligence leads. Perry's smart enough to figure that out."

Kay eyed Tory with increased interest. That was the most the agent had said at any given time since they'd met two days ago. "She is."

"You look beat. Hugh's making a fresh pot of coffee. Smell it?"

"Smells good."

"Join me in a cup?"

"Yeah, I think I will."

"Be right back."

Tory left the office and Kay dragged herself to the vinyl sofa across from the desk. She lay there hoping she'd fall asleep, but too many thoughts swirled in her brain.

"You look exhausted. This might help," Tory said, leaning over Kay with a cup of steaming coffee. She slid the chair next to the sofa and sat down. Gazing out the window, she said, "Looks like rain. Clouding up out there."

"Yeah. Guess I was a day early with my forecast for rain. But that's a good thing since we'd have been hiking in it all day. Actually, we need rain. It's been a dry summer by Alaska's standards. People forget that most of Alaska is a temperate rain forest."

Resting her feet on the arm of the sofa, Tory lit a cigarette. "You live in Anchorage?"

"That's right."

"You have family?"

"Do you care?" Kay asked coldly. "Can't imagine my personal life would interest you." She regretted the hostility as soon as she unleashed it. It was fatigue talking.

Tory seemed unfazed by the comment. "Not supposed to. Least I've been trained not to. You seem like an interesting person, and I thought it'd be nice to talk. I apologize. Shouldn't have asked." Tory stared at Kay for moments that seemed like minutes—like Kay was a rare museum painting up for auction. Then suddenly Tory averted her eyes, leaned back in the chair, and took a long drag from her cigarette.

"I live with two friends."

Tory nodded, pulling her jacket up around her neck. "Cold in here. Haven't got any family. Move around too much."

"Does that bother you?"

"Didn't used to. Does some now. Must be getting old." Tory ran her fingers through her hair, closed her eyes, and took another drag on her cigarette. "Still, I can't imagine settling in any one place for too long. At least not now."

"What did you do before you got this assignment? Can you say?"

"Designed aircraft."

"Wow. That's sounds really interesting. Did you like it?"

"Hell, I love working on cars—fiddling with the engines, anything mechanical. Designing things was great but put me inside the plane, in the guts of it, and I was really in my element. So to appease me, my employers let me tinker with scrap. Most people would go to the movies on the weekend or out to eat with friends. My favorite thing to do was drive to this old hangar where they kept decommissioned aircraft. I'd sit inside an old engine assembly of a large jet, lay out all my tools, and take the guts of it apart, then put it back together. That's what I did on the weekends to relax. Crazy, huh?"

"Sounds a bit unorthodox."

"You like what you do?"

"Most of the time. Don't really like the politics of it. But it doesn't seem like you can separate the environment and politics anymore. Kind of scary."

"It is. Not sure I'd care for your job. Gotta be a people person to do it. I like solitary jobs. Even when I was designing, I worked out of my apartment whenever I could."

"What about what you're doing now?"

"Most of it's solitary. The art of not being noticed," Tory said, laughing. "Perfect job for me."

"So tell me more about being a rogue agent. What does that really mean?"

"A rogue gets trained by the best agents in the world and then waits for one call and one job. When that one job is done, a rogue's life as a viable agent is over. The job might last for days, months, or years. When this job is done, I retire from the field to a desk in Washington. Disappear into an average existence."

"What if the call for that one job never comes?"

"That's also possible. In that case, life is what it is."

"Hell of a way to live. Waiting for the phone to ring."

"Mine rang. So now I get the job done and I don't have to wait anymore."

Kay hesitated, and then asked quietly, "You ever kill anyone before last night?"

"No. And all the training in the world doesn't prepare you for it." Tory leaned forward and said, "Listen, I had a background check run on that security guard. He was an illegal alien—no visa, passport, nothing. Long history in the CIA database though. Found out his country of origin."

"Where?"

"Egypt."

It rained on Saturday as Kay predicted—and then it rained for the next three days. The rain came in torrents and tourists were nowhere to be seen—holed up in their campers or tents, trying desperately to stay warm and dry. The tourists with inadequate supplies and shelter ventured into the main ranger's cabin each morning and were welcomed by Hugh with warm coffee and granola bars. Carla and Russ, dressed in ponchos and fighting not only the rain but high gusts of wind, tried to keep the campsite's main road from becoming impassable by shoveling gravel onto the packed dirt. Eventually, after two days of back-breaking work they abandoned the project when the creek overflowed and finally put gravel and road underwater. The road was impassable to all but those with off-road vehicles.

Kay called Tammy, instructing her to stay put in Anchorage. "No deliveries for the next couple of days. The forecast looks pretty bad through Wednesday. But I'll call you every day with an update. No one's getting in or out of here right now unless you happen to have an ATV."

"So you're stuck there with a grumpy Russ and a macho CIA agent," Tammy observed coyly.

Thinking of the time Russ was getting to spend with Carla, Kay replied, "I'm not sure how grumpy Russ is, and I'm beginning to develop somewhat of a rapport with our agent friend. So it's not quite that bad."

"She must be cute then."

"Say what?"

"The agent—she must be cute. I mean if you've already got a rapport," Tammy said sarcastically.

"You're nuts."

Tammy chuckled. "Just trying to razz you a little. Someone has to."

"I'm glad you've taken on that heavy responsibility."

"You can always count on me. I'll wait for you to call me tomorrow. I've got the maps. They're all packaged up and ready to go."

"Great. Call you tomorrow."

Kay stared at the receiver and shook her head. Tammy was a piece of work but she did keep Kay smiling. Not hesitating a second longer, Kay dialed Lela's work number.

"Hey, babe. Where you been?" Kay asked.

"In your heart where I have always been. Have you not heard my spirit calling out to you across the mountains?"

"No. The only thing I've heard consistently is the buzzing of mosquitoes in my ears and the sound of rain."

Lela laughed, but there was an edge to her voice. "Kay, I have been worried. When Alex said you called, I was relieved but still worried. Is everything all right?"

"We've been doing fine, except for the weather. Right now we're holed up at Riley Creek waiting out the monsoon."

"Then you are safe. My dreams of you have been troubling."

Kay smiled into the phone. Lela had a thing about dreams. She believed that they carried messages from the spirits foretelling the future, both good and bad. "Now listen. There's nothing at all to worry about. How's Al doing? I spoke with her on the phone, but she'd say she was fine even if she wasn't. Is she fine?"

"Yes, she is. She's been cooking up a storm and taking long walks down at the inlet."

"You mean I've been gnawing on Slim Jims and you've been eating gourmet meals prepared by chef Chambers?"

"Absolutely. We've been roughing it here." Lela chuckled. "That was cruel. But I could not resist."

"This morning I had a granola bar for breakfast and a day-old doughnut as an appetizer."

"I won't tell you what I had."

"Thanks."

"When will you return to us?"

"Unfortunately, we have to go back after this weather front passes. We need to get more water samples," Kay lied. "Never got far enough north on the Nenana. We need to get back up there and finish what we started. Probably another week at least, if not longer."

There was a slight tremor in Lela's voice. "Be careful on the river, Kay. Especially after the heavy rains."

"I will. Don't worry."

"That is impossible. I love you, Kay."

"Love you, too." Kay hung up the phone and rested her head in her hands. Dreams and spirits seemed out of place in this world of wilderness and CIA intrigue.

"Must have been talking to someone important," Tory said, standing in the doorway behind Kay.

Kay swung around, startled by the intrusion. "Jesus, you scared me."

"Didn't mean to. Wanted to find out if you were game to go make a supply run. Government Jeep's the only vehicle we can get down that road. Carla says it's all gassed up and at the rate we're feeding tourists, we may starve before the rain lets up."

"Where's the closest camp store? I don't remember."

"Carla says there are two about three miles from here. Located off George Parks so most of it's highway once we get out of here."

"That sounds about right. Trying to get away from all the people?" Kay asked, smiling.

"Hmmm. You're getting to know me far too well, Kay. That won't do. C'mon."

The Jeep growled in low gear as Tory negotiated the flooded road. Tory said something, but Kay could barely hear her above the roar of the wind and slamming of rain against the roof of the Jeep.

"What?" Kay yelled.

"Maybe we should get the food and keep going. You think they'd really miss us?" Tory grinned and, keeping one hand on the wheel, used the other to grab a cigarette out of her coat pocket.

"Russ would miss the food but probably not us. Say, are you going to drive this thing with one hand? Don't you have to shift?"

"Maybe you could light it for me. If you're that worried, I mean," Tory said with a wink and a grin.

The Jeep hit a rut in the dirt road and Kay bounced so hard she hit the roof. "Jesus, we're gonna die out here. Where are the matches?" Tory pointed to her inside breast pocket and Kay carefully reached inside, managing to grasp the matches with her fingertips without getting too personal. Kay lit the cigarette that dangled from Tory's mouth.

Tory smiled and nodded, that same wide grin plastered across her face. "Thanks."

"You're welcome. Now you can use both hands to drive."

Once they reached the George Parks Highway, the going was a bit smoother, though the rain came in constant torrents, making it difficult to see. A few miles up the road, Kay spotted the camp store on the right.

The store was virtually empty so Tory and Kay made quick work of the supply list that Hugh prepared. Kay made sure to grab every box of Hostess doughnuts she could lay her hands on.

"Kay, how 'bout a beer?"

Kay slid the last box of doughnuts onto the counter and glanced back at Tory who was helping herself to a six-pack from the cooler.

"Miller Lite okay?" Tory was smiling again as she held the beer up for the clerk to see. "Add this to the tab," she said before sitting at the only table in the place, presumably available for campers who wished to inhale a quick hot dog or burrito before enjoying the wilds of Alaska just outside the camp store door.

Kay used her government-issued credit card to pay for the supplies and then joined Tory at the table. She opened a bag of Doritos to go with the beer. "I'd almost forgotten about the gourmet food these camp stores sell. Anything the health-conscious camper might need," Kay said, happily tossing a Dorito into her mouth.

"Cheers," Tory offered, holding up her beer.

"Cheers indeed. It's raining and we've got a break from work. I've always loved the rain, and today's no different."

"Used to live in the Midwest," Tory said. "When it rained in the summer, I'd sit on the back porch and play Risk. It's a board game. Supposed to play it with at least one other person, but I'd play against myself and conquer the world all in one afternoon. Pretty sappy story, heh? But, hell, I was only ten. Kids do that stuff."

"Dream."

"What'd you dream about? As a kid?"

Kay opened another beer. "That my seven-year-old sister would stay out of my hair."

Tory laughed and slapped the tabletop with her hand. "Didn't have any brothers or sisters, which was kind of cool. No one to compete with."

"Kind of lonely though."

"Nah. My dad was my best bud. He was an Air Force man and after my mom died when I was twelve, I just crisscrossed the country as an Air Force brat. Loved it. Could hardly wait until my father got reassigned to a new base. Thought that was the greatest. Exploring a new place."

"Exploring has always been a passion of mine," Kay agreed. "I guess that's why I enjoy my work so much."

"Understood. So, you're in a relationship?" Tory asked. "Sorry, but I overheard the last part of your phone conversation."

"Oh, yeah. That was Lela."

"Tell me about her."

"She's quite remarkable. Full-blooded Inuit, attorney, and advocate for her people with the Bureau of Native Land Preservation. Very smart. Honest and dedicated."

"Sorry this assignment is taking you away from her."

"I miss her, but I've gotten used to it. We both travel across the state quite a bit. We try to make up for the days or weeks apart when we can manage to have an entire weekend together. And you? You have someone in your life?"

"Not right now. Would be difficult to explain my disappearances for months at a time. Not able to explain why."

"That would be tough."

"How long have you and Lela been together?"

"Two years."

Tory popped open another beer. "Ah, so the honeymoon's officially over."

"Well, I've always had pretty disastrous relationships so maybe you're right."

"Find that hard to believe."

"What?"

"That you've had disastrous relationships. You seem like a great person."

"Thanks."

"The last girlfriend I had said being mysterious was a real turn-on for her. We sort of fell into this weird kind of pattern where I'd go away for a couple of weeks on an assignment with the aviation firm, then call her on my cell phone the day I'd come home. She'd surprise me with some really sexy outfit. Candles all over the bedroom so the room was nothing but this seductive glow. Rose petals spread across satin sheets. Light jazz on the stereo. One time she was dressed in leather from head to toe." Tory grinned. "I never forgot that homecoming."

"Guess not," Kay said, feeling her cheeks redden.

"Sorry. Didn't mean to embarrass you."

"I think you did."

Tory squeezed Kay's hand. "No, honest. It's the beer talking. And I don't find small talk easy so sometimes I get myself into trouble. Let's put it this way, I've never been praised for my charming ways."

"Maybe you've been trying to charm the wrong people."

Tory laughed. "Think you hit that nail on the head."

Tory and Kay returned to Riley Creek. The rain continued for the remainder of the day, and Kay became concerned about the worsening conditions at the campsite and the safety of the campers. She and Russ braved the downpour to check on the main campsite and evaluate the need for evacuation. Fortunately, it was at a slightly higher elevation than the road. The majority of the rainwater runoff was spilling across the road away from the main campsite into a forested area and collecting under a grove of black spruce.

Sometime very early Wednesday morning, Kay awoke with a start. It was deathly quiet and Kay realized that the rain had finally stopped. She was sleeping on the same vinyl sofa she had occupied for the last three days. Tory was across the room, rolled up in a sleeping bag. Kay glanced in that direction and noticed the tip of a cigarette glowing in the gray dawn. It seemed that Tory didn't sleep well or much. But she had plenty on her mind, and Kay couldn't fathom that kind of worry. Protecting the lands of Denali and the state of Alaska was one thing, but fighting terrorism on Tory's level was impossible for Kay to comprehend. And yet here she was caught at the very core of it, looking for uranium and yellowcake. Getting ready to hike down into the bowels of the earth to track its origin. Terrorism was taking many new forms, spawning dangers that were inconceivable. Thoughts of those dangers were keeping Kay awake—and so she understood well why Tory smoked cigarettes in the middle of the night instead of sleeping. What kind of thoughts were going through her mind? Did she feel helpless, too? Maybe Kay should take up smoking. Or give up sleeping. She pulled the woolen blanket over her head and forced herself back into a fitful sleep. They would be leaving for Sugarloaf today, and that sobering thought was the last she remembered until morning.

Chapter Four

Before they left Riley Creek that Wednesday morning, the remaining kayak stored in the campsite shed was loaded into Russ's truck. None of them wanted to walk the ten extra miles up the east bank of the Nenana River and then climb Sugarloaf again. Tory would occupy the extra kayak and it would afford them some additional storage space.

Tammy arrived from Anchorage bright and early that morning with the package of printed maps and other documents Tory captured on flash cards while in the mining camp's trailer. The maps showed an extensive network of tunnels that spread outward for miles in all directions out of the Sugarloaf Valley.

"You're not really going into these tunnels, are you?" Tammy asked Kay over a cup of coffee that morning.

"I think we are, yes."

"That CIA agent looks a little rough around the edges," Tammy whispered. "Does she know what she's doing?"

"We better hope so. How are things back at the office?"

"Under control. I lied to Ron about why I wouldn't be at work this morning. I told him Jesse was sick."

Jesse was Tammy's five-year-old son. "Good thinking. He give you any grief?"

"Nah. He sounded happy. I think he wants to sneak around the office while I'm not there."

Kay rolled her eyes. "Swell. Something else to worry about."

"Not really. Everything's locked up. Plus Tom will be in today, and he promised to keep an eye on him."

Kay immediately felt better. About twice a week Tom Barnett, superintendent at Denali, worked at the Anchorage office completing visitation and revenue reports. "That's a relief. Who knows what Ron has keys to? He's probably made copies."

"Sure wish you could get rid of him."

"After this is over with, I may just do that."

"What's in these mines, Kay?" Tammy asked, worry lines etched across her face.

"We don't know."

"Oh, I get it. You can't tell me."

"Sorry. No."

"I'm worried. Mines scare me. My grandfather was a miner in northern Alaska. He told me stories when I was old enough. It's not just dangerous work, it's unpredictable. Anything can happen so please be careful."

It was still early morning when Kay, Russ, and Tory reached the entry point at the Nenana River. The rain was long gone and the sun was shining brightly at water's edge. Kay scanned the river with concern. Swollen from the rain, it was running fast almost to its banks. Gone were the dry, rocky patches that Kay and Russ navigated a week ago.

"This is not a good idea—kayaking north with the river this

rough," Kay said. "First of all, we'll be fighting the current. Second, the rain has strengthened the undercurrent."

Tory was adamant to the point of defiance, standing rigidly, arms crossed in front of her. "Don't have any more time to waste. Three days have already been lost because of the weather."

"So what's a few hours more?" Russ asked. "That can hardly matter. We've got a full day of light ahead of us and can't get into the mining camp until after dark anyway. Hell, I ain't crazy about walkin', but paddlin' against that current ain't gonna be a piece of cake either."

Kay had to agree with Russ. "As much as I hate the idea of hiking an additional ten miles and then climbing that damned mountain again, we cannot navigate this river today. We can wait another day or two until the waters calm, but we can't tackle it like this."

Not wanting to waste another day, Tory finally conceded. Russ opened the truck gate, stored both kayaks on its bed, and drove it into the trees and out of sight. They gathered the supplies they could carry, packed them as judiciously as possible, and began the long trek—following the banks of the raging Nenana through the soggy valley and into the mountains.

By the time they reached the summit of Sugarloaf, settling once again at the base camp they had used before, they were all tired, wet, and irritable. Kay was too exhausted to pitch a tent or eat. She lay in the sun with her backpack under her head and slept for more than an hour before waking up to the bickering voices of Tory and Russ. It was an all too familiar sound. Reluctantly, she got up to see what all the fuss was about.

"I can't leave you two alone for a second. What now?" she asked, peering down at them. They were sitting outside one of the tents, arguing over maps of the Sugarloaf Valley mines.

"I just can't see poking around underground," Russ complained. "Look at these maps. Miles and miles of underground tunnels. No one can navigate this crap. It's impossible."

"Excuse me, but I can navigate the tunnels," Tory countered. "There's such a thing as a compass. Plus, we have the maps."

"You say you can," Russ argued. "But how do I know that? How does Kay know that? And what about these maps? Suppose they're false? We don't even know who you really are and you're gonna drag Kay down into these tunnels with you while I stay behind and do what? Twiddle my thumbs and wait? Not on your life."

Kay sat down on the ground facing them. In a very calm voice she asked, "Tory, what do you think we're going to find down there? What exactly are we looking for?"

"Listen, let me say to Russ's point—the maps are for real. The camera I used was only two megapixels. So I sent them to be enhanced and redigitized. At the same time, they were compared with tunnel maps from this mine prepared years ago by government inspectors. There are some variances. Now, they just started mining platinum here about a year ago so variances would be normal. At least at first glance." Tory unfolded one of the maps and traced a tunnel that ran north from the Sugarloaf valley for about four miles. "This tunnel is new. It's located about three miles from the tunnels that are mining the platinum ore. In fact, it's located in between some old coal veins. That's what was originally mined here back in the 1930s. Coal."

Russ was undeterred and relentless. "You told us that you're some kind of rogue. That nobody knows you exist. So where are you sendin' this stuff, and how are you gettin' this kind of information?"

"Maybe I was too vague in my explanation, Russ. To the government I exist, but I'm only a number. Faceless and nameless with no means of identification but one. Biometrics."

"What the hell does that mean?" Russ asked angrily.

Kay answered. "Biometrics. They have Tory's DNA, retina scan, and fingerprints. And I'm supposing that if something happened and Tory needed to be identified as an agent, that's the only way it could be done."

"Biometrics my ass," Russ grumbled.

"It's true, Russ," Kay said with assurance. "I've been reading about biometrics. In fact, the government's using biometric identification to combat terrorism. People with visas entering the country need a machine-readable passport or another form of biometric identification like fingerprints or a retina scan."

Tory smiled. "I'm impressed, Kay. You're right. The government program you just referred to is the US-VISIT program and it does utilize biometrics. The same form of identification that the CIA has been using to confirm the identity of agents for years now."

"Ain't that somethin'," Russ said. "And that's the only way they can identify you?"

"Correct," Tory said. "I have at my disposal unlimited resources within the government to assist me with this assignment. Drop boxes, secure Internet connections, and phone lines. And other means of contact. We're not working alone, guys. Not by a long shot."

For once, Russ was quiet. He blinked a couple of times, finally absorbing it all. Kay thought he had known before that Tory was legitimately working for the government, but because of their obvious personality clash, refused to give her the benefit of the doubt. Kay and Tory said nothing. They looked at Russ and waited.

"So what do we do now?" he finally asked.

"Can I see that map?" Kay interrupted. "I'm remembering something. Something important. If this new tunnel runs due north out of the valley about three to five miles that would lead in the general direction of an area between Suntrana and Eagle Pass." Kay sent the librarians in her mind to work. Somewhere in her brain there was a file named Eagle Pass. What was it that she knew about that area? "I've got it," she said, snapping her fingers.

"What, Kay?" Tory asked.

"The Eagle Pass Coal Mine. The Trapper Creek Gold and Coal Mine. Remember me talking to you about them, Russ?"

"Yeah, I do. You mentioned both of them last week in your office."

"Eagle Pass and Trapper Creek," Kay said again. "Eagle Pass still mines coal and is operational. But Trapper Creek is an old gold and coal mine that's been closed for years. I wondered before if there was a connection. Now that I see these maps, I'm even more convinced. According to your maps, there are mine shafts and tunnels interconnected across this region. Old coal and gold tunnels that crisscross this area for miles. Underground, you could get from one mining operation to the next without being detected."

Tory smiled. "So you connect one mining operation with another and mine uranium ore without being observed because everything is happening underground. Now the yellowcake processing, that's a missing link. But I agree with you, Kay. It's a great cover."

"Yes, exactly," Kay said. "Tory, you mentioned that there's a new tunnel that runs north. I think we need to head for that tunnel and see where it leads."

"That's the plan then," Tory agreed.

"The whole theory seems plausible to me," Russ offered. "Good going, Kay."

Tory handed Russ a duplicate map. "Are you familiar with the Trapper Creek area, Russ?"

"Yeah, sure."

"Would you be willing to snoop around that mine at the northern end? We can meet here in five days." Tory circled the village of Healy. "You know this town?"

Russ nodded. "Sure do. I'll go back to my truck at Nenana. Take a drive to Trapper Creek and poke around. Healy's a good rendezvous point. It's actually a pretty good-sized town for these parts and there's an airstrip nearby. That's an important fact if the yellowcake's bein' shipped out from Trapper Creek. An airport would come in mighty handy."

Tory seemed pleased. "Today's Wednesday. We'll meet on Monday at five o'clock in the evening."

Early Thursday morning when the sun finally set, Russ was on his way to Trapper Creek, and Kay and Tory were once again making their way down into the valley to gain access to the Sugarloaf Valley Mining property. Once they arrived at the western perimeter of the property, they quickly observed the heightened security they feared. The mining company was crawling with extra security guards armed with rifles.

"Not good," Tory said, scanning the area with night vision binoculars. "Need to create a diversion or we'll never gain access to the main tunnel entrance."

"What kind of diversion?"

"The kind that creates enough chaos to funnel everyone to the same area. Going to head south," Tory pointed. "See where those diesel barrels are stored?" Tory handed Kay the binoculars.

"I see them."

"That's where I'll be. If I'm not back in fifteen minutes, get the hell out of here."

"Okay."

"In the meantime, cut a hole in this fence. We'll need to move fast once things get interesting."

Kay took the wire cutters from Tory. "I'll get to work. Be careful."

Beads of sweat poured down Kay's forehead. The night was cool, but each time she snipped a section of that wire fence, the sound seemed to echo across the valley. It was just her imagination, she kept telling herself. When she was done, she sat in the darkness, listening to the footsteps of patrolling guards, hoping Tory would return before the deadline. She glanced at her watch. Four more minutes. Then she heard a rustling noise in the brush. She held her breath.

"Get ready," Tory said, emerging from the shadows.

"What's going to happen?"

"You'll know it when you hear it. Then we move."

A few minutes later, there was a thunderous explosion. The night sky lit up like the Fourth of July. Tory waved Kay underneath the fence. They followed the fence to the northern entrance and then headed east across the main ore yard, zigzagging between the mountains of discarded dirt and rock. By the time they reached the main entrance to the tunnel, there were no guards to be seen. All had run toward the explosion according to Tory's plan.

Quickly, they entered the main underground tunnel. An elevator took them deep into the chilly darkness. When it *clanked* to a dead stop at the bottom of the shaft, Kay held her breath as the sound echoed through the tunnel. Tory seemed unconcerned. She sent the elevator up and then busied herself orienting one of the maps so they could locate the main shaft that connected with the new tunnel running due north. To reach the new tunnel, they needed to turn east for about a mile and a half. For the first half mile after leaving the main tunnel, the eastern shaft was well illuminated by electrical lighting. But the lighting grew more sparse the farther they traveled until they stepped into complete darkness. From that point, they were forced to depend on their flashlights. They also lost the benefit of following the tracks used to extract the platinum ore inside small rail cars. It was slow going. Kay sensed from her footing that they were following a gradual sloping tunnel that continued east but down. The air became noticeably colder and there were more frequent pockets of standing water. Because the ground was uneven, Kay repeatedly lost her footing, slipping and stumbling into Tory who was walking in front.

"Do we still know where we're going?" Kay asked hopefully. Tory stopped and Kay bumped into her again. Tory grabbed Kay around the waist. Kay could feel Tory's breath against her cheek. "Sorry."

"No problem." Tory consulted the compass hanging from a loop on her belt. The flashlight illuminated its floating needle and numbered dial. "We're still heading east." Tory unfolded a map and studied it. "I'd say another mile until we turn north."

"Okay," Kay responded meekly. "It's freezing down here."

"Yeah, it's damned cold."

Though they were both dressed warmly, Kay felt the frigid air infiltrating her bones. The dampness made the air feel even colder. Sloshing through freezing water wasn't helping. Though her boots were waterproof, the icy wetness numbed her toes.

It seemed like hours and as a means to escape the penetrating cold, Kay forced her mind to wander. She had lived in Alaska all her life and experienced the worst of Alaskan weather. But this underground cold was more biting than any she had ever known. Her thoughts drifted as she tried to put herself somewhere else— out of the cold and away from the darkness. She wondered what Lela would think of her trek beneath the earth. They had shared so much together, it was difficult to comprehend that Lela was far away. Or was she?

The numbers just wouldn't add up. No matter how many times she studied the budget report, fooled with the Excel spreadsheet, or consulted last year's budget numbers, Kay could not make sense of it. There was one hundred and thirty-three thousand dollars and change missing. Somewhere a line item had vanished or been truncated by that silly software Kay had never really understood. Two hours wasted and the report was due to Connie tomorrow morning. Kay looked at her watch. It was six o'clock and there was no end in sight to the torture of numbers that swirled in her brain. If only she could go home and feel Lela in her arms. One look into Lela's eyes would put an end to this madness. Kay shuffled through the sheets of paper in front of her, struggling to concentrate. What was the missing line item, and where had she failed to pick it up?

The door to Kay's office suddenly opened and her frustration vanished at the sight of Lela standing in the doorway. Enhanced by the pale blue sweater she was wearing, Lela's misty gray eyes were even more striking than Kay had imagined in her daydreams. Her long dark hair was speckled with snowflakes. In her arms, she carried two large grocery bags and slid them onto the small round conference table in the corner of the room. Without saying a word, Lela emptied the contents of the bags. Inside was a bottle of Kay's favorite champagne, complete with bucket, ice, and glass flutes. A cheese and veggie tray, cold shrimp, and other assorted hors d'oeuvres were also spread out across the table.

"What's all this about?" Kay asked, nearly speechless.

"I felt your pain and frustration," Lela said nonchalantly. "At home, I was puttering around, not really accomplishing anything. It was restlessness that drew me to you. I knew that you needed me."

Kay shook her head and emerged from behind the desk. She grasped Lela's arm and turned her so she could look into those eyes again.

Lela smiled and threw her arms around Kay's neck. "You called to me in your thoughts. You're struggling with something, and I felt you needed a break."

"How do you know these things?"

"I know your spirit because it is also my own."

"God, I love you."

"I love you too, Kay. I will always be close even if you are far away. That is the way love will be with us. Aren't you going to kiss me?"

"Yes, I am."

Kay tried to hang on to the sound of Lela's voice inside her head but it quickly faded like an echo underground. So much had happened to Kay in the past year. Alex's illness, her father's deteriorating health and then death, an increase in Lela's travel schedule, and now her own preoccupation with work. There were times when Lela felt close no matter where Kay was. But holding on to each other had become difficult and Kay felt suddenly lost and alone. Where was Lela now? Why couldn't she feel her presence in that icy black tunnel?

"It's this tunnel, Kay. This is the new one."

"Say what?" Kay was jarred from her thoughts but felt no surprise after realizing that she still dogged Tory's footsteps in that cold dark mine. The daydream of Lela was a fleeting respite.

"We've found the new tunnel. Going to start north and see where it takes us."

"Wish I could see where the hell we're going," Kay muttered.

She slipped again and clawed at the wall of coal to her right to catch herself. "This is an old coal vein," she said, almost to herself. She directed the beam from her flashlight toward the ground and noticed an increase in the water level. It was up to the middle of her ankles. "Say, where's all this water coming from?"

"Always water in mines," Tory said nonchalantly. "Besides, it's been raining torrents for the last two days, remember?"

"Yeah. I'd almost forgotten. I feel like we've been down here for days," Kay said uneasily.

"We need to step up the pace," Tory ordered.

"Sure, sure," Kay grumbled. "I'll try slipping a little faster."

Ten minutes later, her hands slick and cold, feet completely numb, Kay's right foot skidded out from underneath her and she hit the wall hard. The collision jarred the flashlight from her hand and it disappeared into about ten inches of water. She plunged her hands into the frigid water, frantically searching for the flashlight. The water was dark and deep and her hands came up empty. "Tory, the water. It's still rising. We need to find higher ground. Now!"

Tory stopped and turned. For a moment, they didn't move or speak. The only sounds were of running water—a trickling, pooling sound that seemed to come from above, below, all around them. It was dripping on their faces, swirling around their calves. Tory felt for Kay's arm and gripped it firmly. "Stay close. I should've listened to you before. Damn!"

Kay felt the water currents pushing her against the tunnel wall. "What the hell?" she asked herself. The water was up to her knees and rushing with surprising force. She remembered reading once about people drowning in less than twenty-four inches of water because the sheer force knocked them from their feet. Tory dug her fingers into Kay's arm and pulled her along roughly. She was slogging through the water as fast as she could ahead of Kay, flashlight in her mouth, attempting to read the map and tug Kay at the same time. "We need to get out of this shaft. There should be an old shaft—a dead end about a quarter mile from here. Hurry."

The icy water had reached Kay's belt when they stumbled into the dead-end shaft and Kay was only slightly relieved when they seemed to be moving at a gradual incline. Suddenly, the water surged and pushed Kay farther into the cramped shaft.

"The entire mine's flooding," Kay groaned. "Now what?"

"We wait. Hopefully, the water will subside. A vein must have caved in somewhere because of the recent rains. It's allowed the water to seep into the main tunnels."

"I lost my flashlight."

"One flashlight's better than none." Tory studied the small chamber where they stood, turning a full three-sixty. "Looks like the miners started a new tunnel in here, but the vein must have run out so it was abandoned."

"Tory, the water's rising in here, too. Look." The flashlight confirmed Kay's fears. The water was above Kay's waist and still rising. "Tory, I really don't want to drown. Anything else but drowning. Please do something."

"Look, Kay. This chamber meets an old tunnel up above. See? That's why they stopped digging here. Too unstable."

Kay followed the ray of light where Tory aimed the flashlight and saw a dark shadow, an opening just off a narrow ledge of coal. "That's nice, Tory. But how do we get up there?"

"The water will take us up there eventually. But we'll probably freeze to death before that happens. I'm going to climb up."

"Are you crazy? You can't climb sheer rock."

"Been giving it a good look, Kay. It's not sheer. Think there are enough footholds to make it possible."

"And if you fall and break your neck?"

"Then you'll probably freeze to death, but you won't drown. You'll need to hold my pack and the flashlight. Hand me the rope I've got stashed in there, will you?"

The water was at Kay's shoulders and she was growing more frantic. Taking a deep breath, she hung on tightly to Tory's pack. The water was freezing, and her teeth began to chatter uncontrollably. Convinced she was about to drown, she still watched with complete amazement as Tory scaled the rock wall in front of them. She was as nimble as any small primate, finding usable footholds in what appeared to be a sheer wall of coal.

"The flashlight, Kay," Tory yelled. "I need to see what I'm doing."

Kay held the flashlight tightly in both hands, trying to concentrate the beam against the wall Tory was climbing. Ten minutes later, Tory was standing on the ledge looking down at Kay. Kay was treading water and she could feel the current getting stronger, swirling around her shoulders.

"I'm going to throw you the rope, Kay," Tory yelled. "Tie it through the straps of the backpacks and tightly around your waist. As tight as you can stand it. Ready?"

"Ready."

The rope landed within arm's reach and Kay quickly grabbed it. She did as Tory instructed and then looked up. Tory was sitting down, the rope looped around her own waist, her feet planted firmly on the ledge. "As I pull you up, try to find footholds as you go. Can you do that?"

"Yeah, I can do that."

It was a painstaking process and Kay slipped several times, cracking her knees hard against the sheer rock, scraping her arms, cutting her hands. She held the flashlight in her teeth so she could see the wall in front of her, but the flashlight jumped as her teeth chattered. She looked down and saw that the water level was still rising. She'd have drowned by this time and going down was not an option. She heard Tory grunting above her, straining to pull the rope as Kay struggled to navigate the wall. Finally, out of the darkness, Kay felt a hand dig into her shoulder and then she was on the ledge with Tory's arms wrapped around her waist. Tory held her there, hands pressing into her back, face buried in Kay's hair.

"You okay?"

"I'm fine. Thanks."

"Be careful," Tory warned. "The old shaft behind us caved in so we've basically got this ledge and that's it."

Kay struggled to catch her breath and regain her composure. "Swell. Any more good news? We're a couple of sardines until the water recedes. If ever."

"It will. But you're right. We may be stuck here for a while."

Tory helped Kay stow the backpacks in the small space that remained of the old coal shaft. They tried to find a comfortable sitting position on the ledge. Kay guessed the ledge was about four feet wide and six feet long. It was cramped, cold, and uncomfortable, too dangerous to recline in. They sat back-to-back with their arms wrapped around their knees. That was fine for the first couple of hours until Kay grew dizzy from the cold. Her body shook violently. A combination of wet clothes and the frigid air was causing Kay's body temperature to drop. She was suffering from hypothermia, and she knew it. On a positive note, the water stopped rising about four feet from the ledge where they sat in complete darkness.

Tory seemed fine. Her jeans were wet, but she was holding up well, despite the cold temperatures. "Kay, you've got to get out of those wet clothes," Tory said matter-of-factly. "I've got a long-sleeved shirt and some dry socks in my pack. Plus, we've got the blankets."

"I know," Kay agreed. "I'm freezing to death."

Tory rummaged through the backpacks and dug out the clothes. Kay removed her wet jacket, shirt, socks, pants, and shoes and handed them over her head, one at a time, to Tory. She pulled the dry, long-sleeved T-shirt over her head and it felt like heaven. Gingerly, she eased the dry socks on over feet that were numb but painful—a good sign. Tory slid a wool blanket under Kay's legs and threw another blanket over top of them. Kay leaned against the dark wall and listened as Tory moved behind her, still digging into the backpacks.

"What're you doing back there?" Kay asked.

"Rigging a clothesline with this rope. Going to hang our clothes up so they'll dry. I'm also digging out the Bunsen burner and fuel so we can have some hot coffee. Now, there's a risk involved with that, you know."

"If there's methane gas in here, we're going to blow up."

"Right. But with all this moisture, I doubt it. Plus, this shaft has been closed off for some time."

Kay held her breath as Tory struck the match. Nothing happened but the flicker of a cigarette and then the *whoosh* of the burner lighting. "Couldn't help yourself, could you? Just had to light your cigarette first."

"Yeah, wanted to have at least one more puff before blowing up."

"Very funny."

Kay's body was still fighting the cold in uncomfortable spasms, but the coffee was a welcome relief. Tory would only allow her one cup because they needed to conserve the water.

"Let me see your hands," Tory said from behind. Tory held each hand and gently began to clean the cuts and scrapes with alcohol wipes. "Tell me if I hurt you."

"You're not hurting me."

Tory continued cleaning the wounds on Kay's hands and knees, resting her head on Kay's shoulder, flashlight dangling in her mouth as she worked. "There. I've got some bandages in the first aid kit. Hang on a second."

"Were you a doctor in another life?"

"No. But I do have training in first aid."

"You're a woman of many talents."

Kay was sorry when Tory finished applying the bandages, turned off the flashlight, and extinguished the Bunsen burner. The glow of the burner faded and left them in complete blackness. Chewing on some Slim Jims, Kay was unable to see her own hands in front of her face. In the darkness, she heard Tory breathing, along with the trickling sounds of water below.

"You able to sleep?" Tory asked.

"Don't think so. With my luck, I'll tumble off this ledge head-first into the water."

"No you won't."

Kay felt Tory's legs wrap around her own and Tory's arms lock around her waist. "Lean back and go to sleep. I won't let you fall."

Leaning back, Kay rested her head on Tory's chest. "Thanks."

"No problem. Can't have you taking a plunge, leaving me up here alone."

"Yeah, that would be a tragedy. You'd have the food and water to yourself."

"That's not nice. I'd rather share it with you."

"Sorry. I'm a bit unglued, to say the least."

"Understood. Mind if I smoke another cigarette?"

"No. But don't use all the matches."

"Brought extra. That's a phobia of mine. Not running out of matches to light fires and Bunsen burners. But to light cigarettes."

"We all have our priorities."

"I had a girl once," Tory said, snickering. "She was a smoker, too. We were pretty poor then and cigarettes—well, you know they're damned expensive." Tory struck a match and Kay saw the watery shaft again for one brief moment, the dark walls still trickling with moisture. Every time Tory inhaled, the cigarette tip's red glow brought welcome light, if only for an instant. "Anyway," Tory continued, "that inevitable day came when we were down to our last eleven cigarettes and there was no money. None until the following Monday. Being as it was Saturday, this was a crisis for two women addicted to nicotine. To make matters worse, we had an uneven amount. No splitting them down the middle—someone was going to get an extra."

"That must have been some drama."

"You bet."

"You shared the last one, right?"

"Not exactly. I struck a deal with her."

"What was that?"

110

"She was kind of horny that night," Tory chuckled. "So I told her that I'd fuck her brains out *only* if I could smoke the last cigarette afterwards."

"Shit," Kay said spontaneously.

"Do you know she hesitated, like she couldn't decide?"

"Really?"

"Yeah, I guess that's when I knew the relationship was over. When the last cigarette was better than a good fuck." Tory started laughing and Kay joined in.

"You're not going to run out of cigarettes, are you?" Kay joked.

"Well, that depends." Tory tightened her grip on Kay's waist. "I guess it's a good thing you don't smoke. I'd hate to think of the kind of bartering we'd have to do over the last cigarette."

"I'm with you there."

Kay didn't remember falling asleep. During the night or day or whatever it was in that black hole, she did remember finally being warm. There was an odd sensation of feeling protected or watched over. Of suddenly not being alone. This seemed ridiculous since she was not one to admit vulnerability under any circumstances—even to herself. When she woke up, she had no idea how long she slept or what time it was. The first thing she saw was the eerie red glow from Tory's cigarette. Kay wondered if Tory had stayed awake all the time she was sleeping. Awake and smoking cigarettes.

"Did you sleep at all?" Kay asked, attempting to sit up. She was stiff and sore.

"A little. Mostly, I listened to you snore."

"Geez, thanks."

"Oh, it wasn't bad. Though a couple of times I worried about the place caving in from the vibration."

"Aren't you just full of yourself this morning—or whatever the hell it is."

"It's one o'clock Friday afternoon."

Kay did a quick calculation in her head. She had slept for eight hours. "Guess I was tired."

"Hypothermia will do that to you. You needed to rest." Tory cleared her throat. "And I have to say that I enjoyed the company. It's been a long time since I've had anyone sleeping close by."

"Find that hard to believe. An attractive woman like you must have plenty of girlfriends. You certainly have enough stories to tell about the women in your life."

"Stories. Sure. Old history. Like I said before, it's hard to maintain relationships when you're moving around. Been moving around a lot for the last year and a half."

Kay felt Tory's chest rise and fall slowly in silent resignation. "I'm sorry."

"Oh, I've had some flings. Some one-nighters here and there. But that's not really what anyone wants, ya know?"

"Of course not."

"Notice anything?" Tory asked.

"Not really."

"Except for our conversation, it's pretty damned quiet in here."

Kay listened for a moment and realized that Tory was right. She no longer heard the sounds of running water. "Did the water level drop?"

"It did. Take a look."

Tory pointed with her flashlight and Kay leaned over the ledge. There was only a few inches of water left in the shaft. "Thank God. I hated the thought of drowning in this God-forsaken hole."

"Not on my list of favorite things to do."

"Your quick thinking saved my life early this morning. Thank you."

"My pleasure."

"Guess we better get moving."

After a breakfast of Slim Jims and coffee, Tory and Kay used the rope to navigate back down from ledge to floor. Quickly, Tory had them traveling down the main shaft, negotiating their way north. They slogged through the few inches of water that remained, stumbling and slipping until the shaft took an upward turn. Kay estimated they walked another mile before glimpsing an eerie glow in the distance.

"Electric lighting," Tory said softly. "We're getting back to an area where this shaft is being used." They continued for another mile, making better time in the well-lit tunnel. Suddenly, Tory stopped and put up her hand. Kay slipped to an abrupt halt and waited. She felt a strange sensation—a kind of odd vibration beneath her feet.

"Do you feel that?" Tory whispered.

"Yeah, and I can hear it, too. A whirring sound. Like a generator or something. Maybe an electrical generator for the lights?"

"Think it's something bigger than that. Slow and quiet now. Let's go."

Kay noticed that the tunnel continued to wind on an upward grade. Soon the walls were constructed of concrete instead of timbers and coal. She also felt warm air currents. Then Kay heard voices and Tory motioned for her to stop again.

"Voices. Up ahead there's a steel door on the left side of the tunnel. See it?"

"I do."

"Looks like there's another door on the right directly across. I think that's where the voices are coming from. Stay here. I'm going to take a look."

Kay crouched in the shadows as Tory slowly inched her way up the tunnel. For fifteen minutes she fidgeted, praying that Tory wouldn't get caught and wondering how Russ was making out at Trapper Creek. They were three days away from finding out—if they ever managed to get out of this mess. Tory returned and signaled for Kay to move farther back down the tunnel.

"Some kind of processing operation going on here, that's for sure," Tory explained. "If you ask me, whatever that vibration is, it's a large underground generator that's being used to refine ore.

There are two guards located in an office across from the larger room. The door to the processing room is restricted. Key pad access. On this end, next to the guard office, there's another door. I think it may be some kind of storage room. This is all guesswork of course, but I want to get into that storage room. Should be some kind of shift change this afternoon if I'm guessing right. That's when we'll try for the storage room. That door's got a regular lock, ripe for picking."

Kay digested Tory's guesswork. "An underground plant for refining ore. That's interesting. I remember reading about a state-of-the-art underground uranium processing plant that the government built in Montana. Legitimate of course. Supposed to cut down on pollution and cause less visible damage to the environment above ground. But you still have to dispose of the heavy metals used in the processing operation. Heavy metals laced with radiation."

"Yeah, and if you're not the U.S. government and you don't give a damn about the environment, you dump the stuff where no one will find it."

"Or bury it until it accidentally contaminates the underground water table, seeps into the Nenana River, and makes an Inuit fisherman sick with radiation poisoning."

"Right-o."

At ten minutes to three, Kay and Tory moved back up the tunnel closer to the security office. As Tory guessed, the two guards left the office at precisely three o'clock. They shuffled up the tunnel and could be heard talking to the guards who would presumably be taking their place on watch duty. The voices were loud and laughter could be heard. Without wasting a second, Tory and Kay scurried up the tunnel to the room they guessed was used for storage. To Kay's astonishment, it took only seconds for Tory to pick the lock. In less than a minute, they were inside the room, door closed behind them.

Their flashlight illuminated a room that was home to endless rows of metal file cabinets and shelves filled with supplies. At the far end of the room, there were more shelves stocked with large bottles and sealed containers.

"I'm going to check out the files," Tory said. "Make a list of everything that's on that shelf. Find out what's in those bottles and containers."

Kay nodded. With nothing to write on, she would have to make a mental list. There were a couple of lights dangling over the shelves for anyone needing to get supplies. Kay scanned the container labels. There were a variety of acids, chlorides, and alkalis, along with sodium and ammonia. The names of chemicals started to blur in her mind and she found herself starting over, frantically trying to memorize the solutions.

"You got it?" Tory asked.

"I think so."

"Good, because I'm running out of space on my flash card and I have a few more files I want to photograph. Mind keeping an ear out at the door for those guards?"

"No, I'm done here."

Kay stood guard until Tory finished snapping pictures of folders, maps, drawings, and other documents. After listening for a few more minutes at the door, Tory slowly opened it and peered into the tunnel. Hearing nothing, they headed back down the tunnel in the direction they had come from that morning.

Four hours later, they arrived at the original shaft entrance and the elevator to the surface. The elevator was in motion and on its way down. Kay saw six legs through the elevator's metal gate. Instinctively, as had become her habit, Tory grabbed Kay by the arm and dragged her behind some barrels and boxes stacked about twenty feet from the elevator shaft. They listened as the elevator *clanked* to a stop and the cage door opened. Three men in hardhats stepped off the elevator and paused to discuss some documents. Kay was able to hear their discussion clearly, word for word.

"The shipment of waste is scheduled for tomorrow. Looks like the trucks are leaving at eight o'clock."

"What's the current ore processing rate?"

"Rick will have that report. Right now, we need to check the main shaft. Apparently it was flooded yesterday."

Boot scrapes could be heard as the footsteps continued away from the elevator and down into the main tunnel.

"Think we're stuck here until it gets dark," Tory said, her voice edged with frustration. "That's about four and a half hours from now."

Kay sat down and sighed. "Great. Another four hours stuck down here and who knows when those guys will be coming back."

"I'm hoping they leave before we do. The less people around when we take that elevator up, the better."

"Problem is, we're supposed to meet Russ at the northern end of that new tunnel. He's going to be waiting for us."

"Couldn't go out that way past the guards. Had no choice but to retrace our steps."

"Agreed. The only alternative we have is to walk back to Nenana and follow the river back to Riley Creek. We can borrow the Jeep and then meet up with Russ in Healy."

"That'll work. We've got a couple of days before we're supposed to meet him. At Riley Creek I can get these photos uploaded and sent out so we know better what we're up against."

"Works for me. But I'm pretty sure you're up against an underground uranium processing plant. Those chemicals I made a mental list of are all chemicals used in the processing."

"I agree. And while other plants of this type, like the one you mentioned in Montana, are legitimate with the goal of protecting the environment, this underground plant's main objective is to remain undetected. The plant in Montana enriches the yellowcake for use in nuclear reactors. This one's shipping the yellowcake out of the country for sale in the Middle East. Once it's enriched, they'll use it for weapons."

"Nuclear weapons."

"Afraid so."

"And the toxic waste that they're shipping out of here is definitely being dumped illegally. My guess is above the Nenana."

"I suspect you're right about that, too. Hope we can get the hell out of here soon. Don't relish spending another night in this mine."

Kay was surprised. Tory sounded spooked and that was uncharacteristic. But Kay had no intentions of spending another night down there either. "We'll be out of here tonight, even if I have to dig a new tunnel with my bare hands."

"I like your spirit," Tory replied.

As they sat scrunched up behind those crates for the next four hours, Kay couldn't help thinking that Tory seemed to like her spirit just a little too much. She had been getting these vibes from Tory, beginning with their night snuggled together in that bleak, dark hole. Kay reminded herself that the snuggling was necessary—even life-saving. But it was also familiar in a way that transcended their professional association. Professional association? That was a joke and Kay knew it. Something happened to them down in that blackness that changed everything, even if on the surface their relationship appeared to be the same. What were her own feelings? A nagging disconnect from Lela wasn't helping her sort through the confusion. The fact that she needed to question her feelings frightened her more than the sooty underground tunnels that closed in around them.

Chapter Five

Riley Creek was above water and swarming with tourists by the time Kay and Tory returned late Saturday morning. While Tory was holed up in the office at the computer, Kay went in search of Hugh. She found him cleaning up the picnic area, which had been flooded by the rain. After a brief conversation, she reserved use of the station's Jeep for the next several days. The next item on Kay's to-do list was a hot shower. Fortunately, modern plumbing was available in the ranger station on the second floor, and Kay was able to rid her body of the remaining soot and grime from the underground tunnels. After emerging from the mines and hiking back to the Nenana, Tory and Kay stopped at the river's edge to wash the coal dust from their hands, arms, and faces. But the river water was freezing and Kay only lasted about ten minutes. The soot was still everywhere, and Kay was happy to see it swirling down the shower drain in streams of hot water.

Stopping by the office, Kay found Tory moving between the computer and phone. Reclining on the sofa, Kay closed her eyes but never fell asleep. As she lay there listening to the staccato of Tory's typing and an occasional inaudible phrase grunted by Tory into the phone, Lela and Alex dominated her thoughts. As soon as she was able to have the privacy of the office, she intended to call them both.

"Kay, you asleep?"

"No."

"Didn't think so." Tory pulled up a chair. "Listen, I've gotten some preliminary information on those documents I photographed in the storage room. The rest of it's going to be sent later this evening. What we discovered down there was definitely an underground uranium processing plant."

Kay sat up, affording Tory her full attention. "So, we were right."

"We were. The chemicals you memorized are all ones used in the refining process. Yellowcake is being shipped out of there and you were right on, Kay. The way it looks, it's coming out the other side of the mine at Trapper Creek—a mine that's supposed to be closed down."

"Any idea who's running this operation?"

"I've traced some of the documents, phone numbers, and other contacts to Montreal."

"Canada?"

"Yeah, Canada. Can you believe it?"

"Nothing the Canadian government knows about."

"Hell, no. I think a bunch of French Canadians are doing their own thing—basically, an 'up yours' to the U.S. they love so well."

"Maybe this explains their opposition to the U.S. being in the Middle East. The French are making some money on the side."

"Could be. Doubt the French government is officially involved. My best guess is that it's an independent operation, but you never know."

"What's the next step?"

"Meet Russ in Healy on Monday and take a ride to Trapper Creek. Want to see how the stuff is coming out of there, how it's being packaged and shipped. Need to get some more photos—then maybe we can trace this stuff to Montreal and put an end to it."

"Jesus. Not only are they leaking radiation into the Alaskan environment, but they're shipping uranium overseas."

"Yeah. As we know, there's only one step between yellowcake and weapons-grade uranium."

"As for the radiation at Nenana that made the Inuit fisherman sick, it must be coming from the waste they're shipping out of the valley. Like I said before, they must be dumping the stuff above the Nenana River. You've got to get rid of the chemical waste some way if you don't have an aboveground collection pond."

"When this is all said and done, Grace needs to order an EPA team into the Nenana and Sugarloaf areas to do some evaluation and cleanup."

"When can I give Grace an update?"

"As soon as I leave for Montreal."

"You're going to Montreal?"

"Once we're done at Trapper Creek, I'll have to."

"Fine. I guess Grace can wait a few more days."

Later that evening, when the August sun was dipping into the horizon, Kay and Tory sat on the back porch of the ranger station listening to the beautiful silence. To ward off the ever-present mosquitoes, they sprayed themselves with DEET. After a few beers, the hovering mosquitoes didn't matter anymore. The campground was quiet, though the glow of scattered lanterns was still visible in the distance. The night sky was clear, and the stars shimmered, a lighted canopy for the hills and mountains in the distance.

"There's nothing as beautiful as Alaska," Tory observed, cracking open another beer. "I've been all over the world, and there's nothing like this anywhere."

"You really feel that way?"

"Absolutely. When I finally retire from this insanity, I'm going to find a nice, quiet fishing village where I can enjoy the solitude. I'll fish every day, clean them up, and cook the fillets over an open fire every night. With my smokes and beer, won't need another damned thing."

"Sounds pretty good to me."

"If it happens."

"Why wouldn't it?"

Tory took a long sip of beer. "Ah, you never know what will happen with the business I'm in. But you can't worry about it. Just deal with it."

"You mean the danger of it?"

"Yeah. But there's danger involved in your work, too. You must have thought about it. Don't you sometimes find yourself living moment to moment?"

"It's not that intense. But you're in a different ballgame. A different league."

"Must be the reason I like it. Makes you appreciate life."

Tory rolled a sleeping bag onto the floor of the office and then checked the computer one last time. Kay took her same spot on the sofa.

"Any word?" Kay asked.

"We'll have more information later this morning. Taking longer than expected."

Like other nights they shared in the same space, the glow of Tory's cigarettes cut into the darkness. Not able to sleep, Kay replayed the conversations she had earlier Saturday afternoon with Lela and Alex. Lela was relieved to hear from Kay even though she had been busy with work, trying a court case in Juneau. Alex was about to finish the last round of chemotherapy as soon as Lela returned from Juneau. She was more than exuberant anticipating the end of that ordeal. She even talked about looking for a part-time job, though she wasn't sure exactly what that would be. "Maybe I can do some cooking at one of the local restaurants. I'm still licensed." That was one of Al's dreams—to be a chef in her own restaurant. It was the only reason she had worked in plastics research for so many years. She was saving all of her overtime pay for the day she planned to open her own restaurant. Kay was buoyed by the excitement in Al's voice. It was comforting to hear her talk about something unrelated to cancer.

"You still awake, Kay?"

Startled, Kay sat up and caught a shadowy glimpse of Tory kneeling on the floor next to the sofa. "You scared me, for God's sake. I didn't hear you get up."

Tory laughed. "Stealth is part of my job."

"Well, you don't have to be stealth-like around me."

"Sorry. It's just that I had this urge to kiss you."

Before Kay knew what was happening, Tory was kissing her. *Shit* was the only word that popped into her head. And then the kiss was over and a silence hung in the air like humidity on a hot southern day.

"You upset?" Tory asked, intertwining her fingers with Kay's.

"Kinda, yeah. What the hell was that?"

"You're attracted to me, aren't you?"

"I never said that!"

"I didn't say you *said* it. You don't have to say it. I can feel it."

"Oh, really?" Kay let go of Tory's hand. Being in a reclining position with Tory so close suddenly seemed unwise. Standing up, Kay stubbed her toe on the bookcase near the window. "Shit!"

"You okay?"

"I've been better."

"Are you saying that you're not attracted to me?"

"I'm not saying anything," Kay replied briskly. "I'm in a relationship, and you know that."

"So I've heard."

"So, what the hell? You just go ahead and kiss me in the middle of the night?"

"*Shhh*," Tory whispered.

"Yes, let's not wake the tourists and have a scandal," Kay said, rubbing her throbbing toe.

Tory started to laugh. "You are something, Kay Westmore. I do really like you a lot."

"Listen, I like you, too. But like and love are two different emotions."

"Why don't you sit down, Kay? I'm not going to pounce on you."

"That's a relief to hear." Kay sat down, now keeping a close watch on the glow of the cigarette and the movement of the shadowy figure in front of her.

"We're not getting married, Kay. All I said was that we're attracted to each other. It's obvious."

"You didn't *say* anything. You got up in the middle of the night and kissed me. And I know we're not getting married—but I suppose a roll in the hay is what you're used to and all you care about."

"That's not all I'm interested in," Tory said quietly. "I'm interested in you. In the connection we have. Can't you at least acknowledge that connection?"

"All right. I acknowledge that I feel something for you, Tory. But that doesn't mean I'm going to act on it. And you're not going to, either."

"Then why kiss me back?"

"Because it happened so fast that my mind went dumb. Seriously dumb. And it won't be happening again."

Tory gently brushed Kay's cheek with her hand. "Whatever you say."

"Thank you." Kay heard Tory rearranging her sleeping bag. The cigarette was extinguished and the room quiet again. But Kay's mind exploded like an atom bomb. Thoughts raced out of control. She was angry with Tory. Angry with herself. The fact that she was attracted to Tory and stupid enough to admit it was plenty to fuel the self-directed anger. The fact that she couldn't explain the attraction or deny it to herself brought another hailstorm of thought. Just what was she thinking? Had she lost her mind or something? The fact that she was even thinking about Tory made her feel like a cheat. She had been cheated on in past relationships and knew how awful it felt. She regretted not slapping Tory in the middle of the kiss but was so surprised that by the time she knew what was happening, it was over. Or was that just an excuse? Did she like the kiss? Even want it to happen? Shit, what a mess.

Sunday morning Tory acted as though nothing had happened and Kay followed her lead. Anything to avoid another uncomfortable confrontation, especially since Kay still felt confused about what happened and how she really felt about it.

Since they weren't supposed to meet Russ until Monday, Kay and Tory decided to remain another day at Riley Creek. Tory needed more time to scrutinize the documents and information they had obtained about the underground mining facility. Kay decided to use the time to study the planned upgrades at Riley Creek. About an hour into her review of the upgrades, Hugh interrupted.

"Kay, you've got a phone call. From Tammy at the Anchorage office. When you're done with the call, I'll need to talk with you about a little trouble we had last night at the campground."

"Sure thing, Hugh." Kay grabbed the phone in the office. "Tammy, what's up?"

"Listen, I though you'd want to know that Ron's missing."

"Missing?"

"Yeah, he was supposed to be in the office on Thursday but never showed up. Never showed up Friday either. Didn't really think too much about it since he disappears all the time. But then

I got a voicemail message late Friday. It was Ron. He said he wouldn't be in tomorrow either. That he got held up at one of the campsites."

"That's crap. His only assignment right now is projecting supply costs for next year. He should be in his chair in front of the computer getting that done for my review when I get back."

"Well, he's not coming in tomorrow. I'll try to reach his cell phone. But I thought you'd want to know."

"Thanks, Tammy. I'll be at Riley Creek for the rest of the day. Call me if you hear anything."

Hugh was waiting for Kay in the lobby. Despite Tammy's news about Ron's unexplained absence, she tried to focus on the present. "What happened last night, Hugh?"

"Looks like bears tore up some campsites. Want to take a look?"

"Yes, I would." Kay followed Hugh out the back door and down the trail toward the campground. "Anybody see these bears?"

"Heard 'em. Plus the tracks are pretty clear. Still muddy from the rain, and that made for some real nice bear tracks."

It was still early morning, and the campground was crowded with tourists cooking breakfast before they began their excursions for the day. The smell of coffee and frying bacon permeated the cool morning air.

The sound of rushing water signaled that the creek was still running high and as Kay and Hugh crossed the bridge into the main campground, the misty spray from the charging water below created a fog-like effect that temporarily blocked the morning sun.

Hugh led Kay to the area where the bear tracks were clearly visible. "Grizzlies, I think," Hugh mused, stooping over the tracks. "An adult and two youngsters from the looks of it."

Kay agreed. The imprints in the damp earth were fresh. At least two adult bears had trampled the area, searching for food. A few feet away, under the cover of spruce trees, Kay found the contents of plastic garbage bags spread across the ground. "Someone forgot to dispose of their garbage properly," Kay said. "We're lucky no one was hurt."

"Yep. Bears can hunt well enough on their own, but they're lazy critters. If they find an easier food source, they'll take it."

"We need to confirm that all of these campers have bear resistant food containers. Nothing should be left in trash bags. When they get their backcountry permits, they're supposed to be issued the containers automatically."

"Yep. Most people are good about using them. But some forget."

"That could cost them their lives. Have Carla help you interview the tourists occupying the campsites nearby. Make sure everyone understands that using the containers is mandatory."

"Sure thing, Kay."

Kay returned to the office and found Tory still hunched over the computer. "What's the latest?"

"Finishing up. Need to make a cigarette run. Come with me?"

"Not back to the camp store."

"Nice day for a drive," Tory said with a broad smile. "Can fill you in while we're on the road."

"You need to quit smoking."

Tory winked. "My only vice other than attractive women."

"I'm not joining you if you're going to behave badly."

"You're no fun."

"Are you going to behave?"

"It's against my nature, but okay."

George Parks Highway was crawling with tourists. Hikers, RVs, SUVs, Jeeps, cars hauling trailers with ATVs, kayaks, and canoes crammed the highway. It was sunny and sixty degrees. The day was perfect for discovering the beauty of Denali.

"Banner day for the Park Service," Tory said, unzipping her window. "Guess this makes you happy."

"It keeps me employed."

"True enough."

"So what did you find out about the uranium mine?"

"Interested in talking to Russ tomorrow and see what he's observed at Trapper Creek. My sources are guessing that the yellowcake is being shipped by truck somewhere—and then flown out of the region. Healy airport is closest so we've got to consider that as a strong possibility."

"There are some airstrips near Denali."

"Also a possibility. But they'd have to do a bit of backtracking and spend a lot of time on the road reaching those airstrips. The more time on the road, the greater the possibility of being discovered."

"Russ may be able to fill in the pieces of the puzzle."

"I'm banking on it."

At the camp store, Tory insisted that they sit at their usual table, which of course was the only table in the place. Kay could only laugh. Grabbing a six-pack, Tory sat down and cracked open a beer for each of them.

"Know what I like about you, Kay?"

"You said you were going to behave."

"I am behaving. What's wrong with telling someone why you like them?"

Kay rolled her eyes. "Okay. I'm all ears."

"You're strong but compassionate. Sensitive. I like that combo. You don't take shit, but you know when to be a lady." Tory shrugged and lit a cigarette. "Can't be the first one to notice these things about you."

"I met you eleven days ago. How do you think you know me so well?"

"Some people are easier to read than others. Me, I'm not so easy to read."

"No?"

"Not supposed to be. Trained not to be."

"So is it hard?"

"Not catching your drift."

"Hard to be mysterious? Aloof, for lack of a better word."

"Not at all. But there are times when I wish I could be myself. Like when I'm with you."

"You're misbehaving again."

"Maybe."

"So are you saying that I can never know the real you? The government won't allow it?"

"What would you like to know?"

"I have my own perceptions about you."

"Now I'm all ears."

"You talked about your dad and how you loved moving around the country while he was in the service. I think that's a pile of crap. No kid likes that. But that sense of independence has served you well in your job. Moving around. No permanent connections." Kay studied Tory's eyes—that deep, almost impenetrable green. "But you want permanence. Want to feel connected to some place or someone. But it's scary to you now. It's scary because you've never had it."

Tory flinched then drained her beer. "You going to hang your shingle out anytime soon, doc?" she asked sarcastically.

"I thought we were exchanging impressions. Or are you the only one who's allowed to do the profiling?"

"Ouch. Okay, you've made your point. And your impressions are accurate. Good job."

"Where are you going to find permanence, Tory?"

"Maybe we could just sit here for the rest of time. I'd go for that." Tory reached for Kay's hand and squeezed it tightly. "You're an amazing woman, Kay. Fate brought us together, and I think I'm falling in love with you."

Chapter Six

Russ was waiting for them in Healy at Denali Lakeside Lodge. He was sitting in his truck, feet propped on the dashboard, eating a ham sandwich and french fries and drinking a Pepsi. Little packets of mustard and ketchup were strewn all over the passenger seat.

"How you ladies doin'?" he mumbled while chewing.

Kay eyed the sandwich. "We're hungry. Where'd you get the food?"

"The lodge has a restaurant," Russ said in between swallows. "Go ahead. I'll wait for you."

Kay stared at him for a moment and then said, "You're not coming in? You're going to sit out here and eat that sandwich in this truck?"

"I was gonna do that very thing before you guys arrived." Russ wiped his mouth on his sleeve. "It's a nice day. Too nice to sit inside."

"Well, how about coming inside and giving us an update on Trapper Creek?" Tory suggested. "We need to sync our information. Plan our next steps."

Russ seemed unconcerned. "I'll join you soon. First I gotta use the lobby phone to make a call."

"Fine. Join us when you're done," Kay said crisply, walking toward the lodge. "We'll be in the restaurant. By the way, you've got mustard in your beard."

"Guess he's hot to call his girlfriend," Tory said, opening the door for Kay. "Must be love."

Kay ignored the comment and asked for a table. Love was one topic she was more than happy to avoid discussing.

"Are you angry with me, Kay?" Tory asked while salting her fries. "You've been awfully quiet today."

"I'm not angry. Just want to finish this assignment and get back to Anchorage and my real job."

"So you can get away from me?"

"That's not what I meant. I'm worried about my friend, Alex. I told you—she's got cancer."

"Yes, I know. I'm sorry. How's she doing?"

"Seems to be doing okay. It's hard being away from her right now."

"And you miss Lela?"

Kay reached over the other condiments and grabbed the ketchup. "Of course I miss Lela," she snapped. "Why shouldn't I?"

"No reason. Wasn't implying that you didn't. It was a declarative sentence, Kay. You're wound pretty tight today."

Kay stabbed at her french fries. "I'm annoyed. Russ is acting like a schoolboy. You're saying idiotic things. And I'm . . ." Kay dropped her fork.

"What?"

"And I'm *thinking* idiotic things."

Tory reached for Kay's hand and gently squeezed it. "Kay, it's all right. These things happen."

"What things happen?" Russ asked, standing over them, eyeing them both with suspicion.

Tory let go of Kay's hand. "Nothing. Just forget it."

"You two certainly are cozy," Russ observed with a tinge of sarcasm. "We still havin' a meetin' or should I come back later?"

"Don't be ridiculous," Kay said quietly. "We need to talk. Tell us what you know about Trapper Creek."

Russ ordered a beer and sat down next to Kay. "I found out that stuff is bein' shipped out of there. That's what."

"How?" Tory asked.

"In trucks marked *Eagle Pass Coal Mining Company*. But I don't think the trucks belong to Eagle Pass. It's some kinda front 'cause I followed one of them and they drove from Trapper Creek right past the Eagle Pass Mining Company to the airport. The guys drivin' the trucks had union-type clothes on and hardhats. They looked like mining company employees, but I'm guessin' they aren't." Russ held up a flash card. "Got some photos for ya."

Tory took the card and pocketed it. "Thanks, Russ. Good work. Can you take us back to the area where these trucks are loading at Trapper Creek? Want to get into the mine from this end and see what's up."

"Sure. After dark?"

"Uh-huh. Early tomorrow morning."

"No problem. By the way, I reserved us some rooms here for the next few days," Russ added, taking a swig of beer. "Wasn't sure how long we'd be here."

"I'm guessing a few days ought to do it," Tory said, pushing her plate away. "That seem right to you, Kay?"

"Yeah, sure. But if we have to be up all night, I'm going to my room. I've got a splitting headache."

Kay lay on the bed with her eyes closed, willing the headache away. In a half-sleep, she thought about Lela and the first time they met. It was in an airport in Barrow, Alaska, in the dead of winter. Lela drove Kay to town in her truck, bouncing over snow and ice-covered roads in temperatures below zero. But Kay didn't remember being cold. All she remembered was staring at the attractive Native American woman who was trying to drive the truck with one hand, while coaxing some heat from the dashboard controls with the other. The memories were vivid to the point where she could still hear Lela's voice—soft, precise, and almost hypnotic. The breakup with Stef was still new and raw when she met Lela, leaving a wound that never healed—not even now as she lay there, her temples pounding. Stef still occupied a space in her heart, despite her best efforts to exorcise that demon. And from where she found the strength to walk away, even when Stef wanted to come back, she would never know. Had Lela given her the strength to move on? There was something exotic about her love for Stef as there was something spiritual about her love for Lela. So where did Tory fit in and why? What was it about Tory that pulled at her gut? Clearly, it was all wrong. Just like it had been all wrong with Stef. A relationship destined to fail and still with the power to pull her in.

She must have fallen asleep until the knock on the door. Kay rubbed her eyes. It was dark in the room, but the clock read nine p.m. Her watch confirmed the time. As she staggered toward the door, she realized that, mercifully, her headache was gone.

Tory stood in the doorway holding two six-packs of Miller Lite, one in each hand. She was dressed in a muscle shirt with no bra, cargo pants, and bare feet. "Thought you could use a beer," she said with a grin. "Can I come in?"

"Sure."

"Must've been sleeping. Did I wake you?"

"Yeah. But it was time to get up."

Tory slid the beer onto the coffee table and plopped down in the recliner like she was there for the long haul. "Already talked to

Russ. Won't be going anywhere tonight. It's teeming rain and the fog is as thick as maple syrup. Can't see a damned thing."

"Well, that explains why it's dark at nine o'clock." Kay sat down on the sofa and propped her feet on the coffee table. "You know, I'm really hungry."

"Didn't finish your lunch. But we can take care of that. What're you hungry for?"

"Surprise me."

"Okay."

While Tory ordered food, Kay took a shower to wake up. Feeling much better, she wrapped herself in the terry robe provided by the inn and sat back down on the sofa. Two room service trays were on the coffee table and Tory was pouring beer into two beautiful pilsner glasses.

"Where'd you get those?"

"Hey, if we're going to have room service, complete with linen napkins, we might as well drink from glasses instead of bottles."

"What's for dinner?"

"Grilled pork chops, garlic mashed potatoes, and asparagus."

Kay eyed Tory with suspicion. "How did you know I love pork chops?"

"Called Russ and asked him."

"What's he doing?"

"He'd already had dinner and was planning on some sack time. Was worried about you and asked if you were feeling better. Told him I didn't know but was betting that a good dinner and a nice, cold beer would do the trick."

"You're right."

"Thought so."

They ate in silence until Kay asked, "Is your dad retired now? From the military?"

"Yeah. Lives in Maine."

"That where you're from?"

"Originally. Like I said, we moved a lot."

"What about your mom?"

"She's with dad. Soul mates, you know?"

"That's nice." Kay finished her beer and Tory poured another. "My parents are both gone now. It's the hardest thing I've ever experienced. At least until Al got cancer."

"That sucks, Kay. Your dad dying, then Al having cancer. Doesn't get much worse than that."

"No, it doesn't."

"You're hurting pretty bad. It shows."

"That much?"

"Yeah. That much." Tory pushed her tray away. "It makes me want to hold you. To stop the hurting."

Kay eased back on the sofa and then suddenly Tory was there, leaning over her, fingertips caressing her face. Silently, she screamed, "No!" But Tory was still there, kissing her, both hands around her neck, pulling her deeper into her mouth. And there she found that erotic power again, that dominating force that took her completely. Not the fire of Lela but the dominance of Tory, which she succumbed to inexplicably.

The bed was cold without her robe, but Tory's body, still clothed, covered her with warmth at the same time Tory's mouth blanketed her with kisses. Kay clutched Tory's shirt. She could feel Tory's muscles ripple beneath the fabric as those strong arms encircled her. There was gentleness in her voice as she whispered, "You're so damned sexy." But no gentleness in Tory's touch, only power and seduction.

Pulling at Tory's shirt, Kay tossed it to the floor. Her skin was soft and deeply tanned. Kay slid her hands over Tory's breasts, up her shoulders and neck to her face. Then she stopped, locking into those emerald green eyes that clearly saw Kay's desire to surrender. And then Tory went down on her, slowly working her to the edge. She wrapped her fingers in Tory's hair and moaned, "Yes, darling. Yes."

Tory stopped and kissed her deeply. "You love me, don't you, Kay?"

"Yes," Kay whispered, her lips caressing Tory's ear. "But I don't know why."

Tory buried her mouth into Kay's neck. "Because there's no gentleness in me. None in you. We're fighters."

All Kay knew was what she felt at that moment—an intense passion that consumed her. When she came in Tory's arms, she felt no distance between them. Whether or not it was love, she didn't know. She felt safe and complete.

Kay rocked to the movement of Tory's hand inside her. When Tory's mouth settled on her breasts, she closed her eyes and bit her lip. Tory put her hand around Kay's mouth forcing her lips open, kissing her, whispering, "Don't hold back on me, Kay. I want to feel you let go. Again and again." With the movement of her hips, Kay forced Tory deeper until multiple orgasms shuddered through her.

Kay held on tightly as the moment ebbed. Being in Tory's arms was raw and real. The way she felt about Alaska. She rolled over on top of Tory, letting what was left of her orgasm run over Tory's stomach. Tory pulled Kay's breasts into her mouth, but this time Kay didn't close her eyes. Instead, she watched her own arousal and held Tory's hand as it slipped inside her once again. Then she watched the hand that fucked her and listened to Tory's voice saying, "I love you." And, for what seemed like the first time in her life, she heard the words.

Tory's cigarette diffused the darkness that had finally settled over the room. At some point, Kay fell asleep in Tory's arms. When she woke to the familiar glow of Tory's cigarette, she was nestled against Tory's side. An arm around her back held her close.

"Tory, what time is it?"

"Uh, two-thirty. Been listening to you snore with the rain as a backdrop. It was nice."

"Did you sleep?"

"No."

"Do you ever sleep?"

"Not much. Once every couple of weeks I really crash."

"That's amazing. I'd be a walking zombie."

"Don't know why, but I've never slept well or much. Always afraid I'll miss something, would be my guess. Or maybe I equate sleep with wasted time."

"For me it's a welcome escape."

"Trying to escape from me already, huh?"

"That's not what I meant."

Kay heard Tory tamp out her cigarette. She turned over and ran her fingers through Kay's hair. "No regrets?"

"Regrets?"

"About what's happened with us."

"I'm trying not to think about it."

"It's a moment in time, Kay."

"I know."

"Then let's not waste any more."

Tuesday morning they met Russ for a late breakfast at eleven o'clock. He had already found a table and was perusing a menu. As Kay and Tory sat down, Russ looked up and eyed them curiously. "You two get any sleep?"

Tory handed Kay a menu. "Some. Blasted downpour kept me awake. Not that I ever sleep well."

"Kay, you look like hell," Russ blurted.

"Thanks a bunch."

"Did *you* get any sleep?"

"Actually, I did. But for some reason I'm still tired. That migraine didn't help much."

"I slept like a baby. 'Cept around midnight I woke up and realized I needed to recheck our supplies. Called your room, Tory, and there was no answer." Russ glared at Tory before ordering pancakes.

Tory ordered cereal and fruit and remained unflappable. "Probably in the shower. Was up late studying maps of the tunnels near Trapper Creek. Since we need to go back into those tunnels, wanted to make sure we know where we're going. We can check the supplies after breakfast."

Russ sipped his coffee, eyes bouncing between Tory and Kay. His mood was beginning to unravel Kay. She tried avoiding his glare, convinced that he knew something happened last night. After breakfast, they checked the remaining supplies in the Jeep and Russ's truck. They were low on flashlight batteries, food, and coffee. Tory volunteered to take the Jeep to the other end of town and pick up what they needed. Kay and Russ stayed behind to organize and repack everything.

"What's going on with you and her?" Russ asked bluntly after ten minutes of uncomfortable silence.

Kay finished rolling her sleeping bag and gave him a sideways glance. "You're in a mood today. What's up?"

"You didn't answer my question."

"Nothing's going on. I just want this assignment to end."

Russ stood up, arms folded, towering over her as she continued organizing her backpack. "Now who's lyin'? You know, a couple of weeks ago, we were still friends. I know you're my boss, but we could always talk. I could always count on you. Then you got after me about Carla. Didn't even give me a chance to explain nothin'. You just judged me straight away and that hurt. I thought we'd gotten past that when we talked that first day climbin' Sugarloaf. But I don't think that conversation meant nothin.' Now you're gonna lie to me about you and Tory. Why? 'Cause now you're standin' in my shoes, but you're too much of a coward to admit it?"

Kay rose slowly, looked him squarely in the eye, and said, "Russ, please. I don't want to talk about this. My mind is swirling and I can't handle a confrontation right now. Okay?"

"Guess now it's my turn to ask the same questions you asked me. How could you do this to Lela? What were you thinking?"

"You're crossing the line, Russ."

"Of what? Our friendship?"

"We need to finish getting these supplies ready," Kay said, her voice trembling.

"What about when you asked me about Carla? That wasn't crossin' the line? 'Cause you're my boss and that gives you the right?"

"You're talking stupid."

"You think I'm stupid? I know you, Kay. Maybe better than anyone else. Better than Alex and Lela even. I can see it in your face—the guilt you feel today. 'Cause you know what? I've felt that same guilt. It only proves one thing—that you're human, too."

"I haven't got anything to say to you."

"Maybe not. And that's okay. But things happen and things change. Sometimes faster than you can think to stop them. You think you got some future with Tory? You're gonna have to answer that question, same as I will with Carla."

"Thanks for the lecture."

Kay threw her gear into the bed of Russ's truck, slamming the tailgate shut. Then she returned to the lodge for another cup of coffee, but mostly to get away from him and the truth. She sat alone at a table near the back window where she could see the imposing mountains in the distance, their peaks shrouded in mist. The lodge was bustling with tourists getting ready for a day of excitement in the Alaskan wilderness. Feeling numb, Kay prayed the coffee would wake her up from what felt like a surreal dream. Russ was right, of course. She had cheated on Lela, violated the trust of that relationship and didn't have a clue why. She only knew that she felt a strong connection to Tory and that it came seemingly out of nowhere to torment and confuse her. It didn't have anything to do with unhappiness or loss of love for Lela. Yes, there were the normal problems of any relationship, but nothing that couldn't be worked out. Maybe Russ was right about things happening too fast to think about the consequences.

"You okay?" Tory asked, sitting across from her.

"Fine. Get everything we need?"

"Yeah, no worries there. But I am worried about you."

"I'm trying to figure out what's happening. Not making much progress."

Tory lit a cigarette, inhaled, and blew the smoke to one side. "Lived in Seattle for a while when I was in my twenties, and there was this very attractive woman about ten years older than me who lived in the townhouse next to mine. At the time, I was living with my current girlfriend, who I adored." Tory drummed the tabletop with her fingers. "One day, while my girlfriend was working night shift at the hospital, the woman next door knocks on the door and asks me if I know anything about VCRs. She's trying to hook hers up and doesn't have a clue. Next thing you know, she's telling me how butch I am and how she's been attracted to me ever since she first laid eyes on me. It was pretty flattering."

"So you went to bed with her."

"Yeah. But it didn't have anything to do with not loving my girlfriend. Guess it was more or less an ego thing. When you get your ego stroked like that, it's hard to control the uncontrollable, you know?"

"Do you have a girlfriend story for every occasion?"

"Pretty much," Tory said with a shrug.

"I cheated on Lela."

"True. You met someone who thinks you're terrific and who's in love with you."

"And my ego got the best of me?"

"Maybe. But I pushed pretty hard." Tory grinned. "And I am kinda irresistible."

"You're full of shit."

"That, too." Tory squeezed Kay's hand. "I don't have any illusions that you're going to give up your life with Lela, Kay. Could be we only have a few days left together. If that's the case, I'm a big girl. I can handle it. It'll hurt, but I can handle it. Can you?"

The gravel and dirt road to Trapper Creek was rain-soaked and rutted. Russ led the way in his truck and Tory and Kay followed in the Jeep. As they approached the old mining camp, Russ pulled off the main road into a small cluster of trees. After unpacking their gear, they walked the last mile until reaching a rocky outcrop that overlooked the original mining site. It was eleven o'clock Tuesday evening. The sun was just beginning to disappear below the horizon. From that rocky vantage point above the mines, Tory trained her binoculars on the area below and scanned what was once the main entrance. From maps they studied earlier, there were many hidden exits from the old mine but only two main entrances. The original entrance ran south then turned west toward Eagle Pass. Another entrance, long ago abandoned to make way for the new shaft, ran east and then turned south again. Many old tunnels ran both east and west, some dead ends, exhausted veins of coal or gold that created a confusing maze linked together by common tunnels. They conferred about the two main entrances, old and new, and the need to investigate each one. Kay was convinced that one of those tunnels was linked to the underground uranium mine and was being used to extract yellowcake. Where and when the shipments were coming out and how they were being transported away from Alaska were the questions that needed to be answered. Russ had seen the trucks but was unable to pinpoint their base of operations. The road below was the road being used to the airport. Tonight they would continue the investigation by entering the mines again.

Tory finished scanning the grounds below and climbed down the rock face to a flat area near the trees where the vehicles were parked.

"There's no activity right now that I can see. Kay's right. We need to check out each entrance—the one here just off the main road and the one farther east."

Russ looked toward the graying horizon. "The rain's over for now and the fog's rollin' in again. But I think that's a good thing. It'll give us some cover on the road."

"And it's doubtful anything will be coming out of those mines tonight. It's one thing to bring out shipments under cover of darkness, but with the condition of the road and this gathering fog, it would be far too dangerous," Kay added.

"Exactly," Tory agreed. "It's our best shot to check out this area undetected. I suggest we split up according to our original plan. Kay and I can take the Jeep farther down the road to the eastern entrance. The road is a mess and the Jeep is the only way we'll get through. Russ, you can check out the entrance just off the road here."

Kay checked her watch. "We'll leave at midnight and meet back here no later than five o'clock."

Tory nodded. "Five hours should give us plenty of time to check out the two tunnels."

"Hey," Russ whispered. "I think we're bein' watched. Just saw the glint of a flashlight in those trees west of here."

"We need to check it out," Tory said, fingering the weapon inside her jacket. "Russ you circle south, around those rocks. Kay and I will circle north through the trees. Let's go."

Inside the line of trees, it was dark and muggy. Kay saw the flash of light again and Tory put up her hand. They stooped and moved quietly, zigzagging from tree to tree. The halo of light was moving toward them. When they had closed the gap to a few yards, Kay squinted into the blackness, barely making out the form of a person. A few moments later she grabbed Tory by the shoulder.

"My God, it's Ron Hadley!" she whispered, head swimming in disbelief.

"Who the hell is he?"

"Works at the Anchorage office. Must have followed us here."

"Why?"

"I don't have a clue."

Suddenly, they heard angry voices. The glow of light hit the ground. Tory and Kay broke into a sprint and found Ron pinned to the ground with Russ's knee in his back.

"Let me up, you bastard!" Ron complained.

"What the hell are you doin' here?" Russ demanded.

Ron glanced at Kay and pointed his finger. "Following her. What are you doin' outside of Denali? Campsite inspections? Yeah, right. Wait until Connie hears about this. Your ass will be fired for sure," Ron growled.

"Shut the hell up," Russ hissed, digging his knee deeper into Ron's back. "You ain't sayin' nothin' to no one."

Tory turned to Kay. "What's with this guy? He have a beef with you or something?"

"I'm afraid so."

"We're going to have to detain Mr. Hadley. Russ, you got any rope?"

"Yeah, I do. In the truck."

"Let's make Mr. Hadley comfortable, shall we?"

Fifteen minutes later, Ron Hadley was hog-tied and gagged under a tarp in Russ's truck. Kay felt a disturbing sense of satisfaction as she peeked one last time underneath the tarp.

"We won't have to worry about him for a while," Tory said. "But I will need to deal with him later."

"What are you gonna do to him?" Russ asked.

"Teach him some manners," Tory answered. "And convince him to keep his big mouth shut."

At half past midnight, Tory cranked the Jeep and attempted to negotiate the muddy, rutted and, in some places, flooded road that led east. Russ proceeded on foot, his navy backpack fading into the misty darkness. With a flashlight, Kay marked their progress on the map. It was slow going as the torn-up road jostled the Jeep like it was made of tin. About a quarter mile from the spot on the map where the eastern mine entrance was located, Tory was forced to leave the road, which was blocked by fallen trees and other debris. Parking the Jeep in the shadows, they continued on foot in the direction of the mine entrance until the sky suddenly disappeared under an overhang of trees. In the pale darkness, Kay squinted at the sky until she realized there was no sky. A canopy of camouflage netting was suspended over what appeared to be the mine entrance.

"Leafy trees in the middle of the tundra. I knew that wasn't right," Kay muttered.

"Great camouflage," Tory whispered. "Prevent detection from aircraft. Would take a very skilled eye to spot this operation."

The road near the old mine entrance had been widened and tire tracks from trucks and heavy equipment were evident. "Someone's been awfully busy here," Kay observed. "Rather elaborate setup."

"And the blocked road turns people away," Tory answered. "But how are they getting the shipments out?"

"Look," Kay said, pointing to an opening in the underbrush just east of the tunnel entrance. "They've built another road out of gravel. It's a turnaround that probably connects to the main road west of where the road is blocked."

"Very clever," Tory said, moving closer to the tunnel entrance. "This project is obviously well funded. But yellowcake sells at a very high bid in the Middle East."

Kay stared at the tunnel entrance, dreading the thought of stepping into the eerie blackness. "This entrance leads to the processing plant. It's obvious."

Black turned to gray as Tory illuminated the entrance with her flashlight. "Let's get this over with."

It was dark, cold, and damp inside and Kay suppressed her panic. Keeping one hand on the rocky wall to her right, Kay tried to maintain sure footing. But once again the going was rough, and they inched along, step by step. Unlike the tunnels at Sugarloaf, these tunnels were cramped and the air stifling. Kay wondered how the yellowcake was being transported out. Not by rail. There were no tracks laid and the tunnels were too narrow for rail cars. It wasn't long, however, before they stumbled on the likely answer.

Tory stopped to check out the mini-forklifts. There were four of them parked end to end about a mile from the entrance. "This is what they're using. These mini-forklift motors are battery powered so they're super quiet. They load the containers on the forklifts, move the stuff through the tunnel and into trucks for transport to the Healy airport."

"From the Healy airport to where?" Kay asked.

"Good question. The planes at Healy are only twin-engine or small jets without a lot of range. If I were to make an educated guess, they're flying the stuff into Canada. Some obscure landing strip in the Yukon. From there they may be switching back to trucks. Then maybe back to planes to Montreal."

"How are you planning to verify the route?"

"By satellite. I'm going to slap a tracking device on their next plane out of here. Then my buddies at the CIA will track the plane to its next destination. Of course, that means staking out the airport and keeping an eye out for Eagle Pass Coal Mining trucks."

"What happens after you find the next airport? In the Yukon or wherever?"

"Keep on the trail all the way to Montreal. After Healy, you and Russ head back to Anchorage and business as usual."

"The Montreal deal. Sounds dangerous."

"Nah. Piece of cake. Let's keep going and see what else we find."

They stumbled in the darkness and stale air for what seemed like hours until the tunnel began to turn slowly south. Another ten minutes later they found an electrical generator supplying power to a now illuminated tunnel. Two more mini-forklifts, stacked containers, and other supplies signaled that they were closing in on the underground uranium processing plant from the opposite direction. Fresh air was being pumped in through ventilation shafts, making it easier to breathe. Tory took photographs with the digital camera while Kay made notations on the maps. The sound of approaching voices startled them. Tory grabbed Kay's arm and headed for the shadows. They ducked behind some crates stacked near the mini-forklifts. In the process, Kay slipped and slid into one of the crates, resulting in a loud *thud*. The voices were suddenly quiet.

Kay held her breath as the pain in her jammed ankle shot up her leg. The footsteps and voices drew nearer until the conversation between two male voices was audible.

"You hear that?"

"What?"

"Thought I heard something. A thump or something."

"Where?"

"Farther down."

Within moments, the footsteps stopped a few feet from where Kay and Tory were hiding. Through a slim crack between the stacked crates, Kay could see a pair of legs standing just inches away.

"You sure you heard something? These tunnels can fool you. Probably just air flow. Everything's an echo through here."

"I don't know. It sounded like something fell. Or someone."

"Getting spooked in your old age?"

"Maybe."

The beam of a flashlight flickered across the tunnel walls, finally falling on the stack of crates that hid Kay and Tory from sight. Moving noiselessly away from the slim crack she was peeking through, Kay clung to Tory to keep out of view.

"C'mon man. Let's get these batteries and head back. I've got some good whiskey in my desk just dying to be opened. Couple of shots in your coffee will cure those nervous jitters."

"I ain't jittery. Just wondering how long we can keep shipping this stuff out of here before someone's hot on our asses. Don't forget Rick got his throat cut and then there was that explosion a few days ago."

"I'm not forgetting anything. This business we're in ain't without risks, though. So long as they keep the money flowing into my pockets, I'm not gonna wimp out or complain."

"Yeah, yeah. Still, this weather sucks. It backs up the inventory. And that makes me nervous."

"C'mon. It's clearing up tomorrow. Good weather means a busy night. Let's go."

Kay listened as a crate was cracked open on the other side of the tunnel. A few minutes later, after the men stacked three of the crates on one of the forklifts, its engine came to life and its headlights lit up the tunnel like a sports stadium. For the first time, Kay was able to completely view the inside of the mine. The main tunnel was about ten feet wide and fifteen feet high with solid rock walls lined with timber supports. Small veins of black coal were visible throughout the tunnel, but there was more rock than coal, signaling the death of a once very productive mine. The sound of the forklift's engine slowly died away, and Kay inhaled deeply, letting out a calming sigh of pure relief.

"That was close," she said, turning to Tory. "Thought my heart was going to fly out of my throat."

"Fortunately, we weren't far from cover. I'm glad the supplies they needed were in the crates over there," Tory said, pointing to the other side of the tunnel. "That was even luckier."

"Now what?"

"We keep going. Want to verify that this tunnel leads to the underground uranium mine we saw last week. Once we do that, I can report without any doubt that uranium is being shipped directly out of the eastern tunnel."

"Can't we assume that now?"

"We can. But that's not good enough for the CIA. After

September 11 things changed. The agency changed. Everything is documented and verified. All leads are exhausted. We don't assume anything anymore."

An hour later, after confirming that the Trapper Creek tunnel converged with the underground uranium processing plant, Tory and Kay emerged into the cool night air. Relieved to be out of the mines, they drove the Jeep back to the original overlook where they planned to meet Russ. It was four o'clock Wednesday morning and they still had another hour before Russ was due back. They parked the Jeep next to Russ's truck. After checking on Ron who was still securely bound and gagged, they got back inside the Jeep to escape the cool night air.

"Russ should've been back by now. He should have beat us back here," Kay said nervously, staring at her watch.

"Maybe he found another tunnel that connects to the uranium processor. The way all these tunnels spiderweb under this valley, it's possible."

"Could be."

Tory pulled Kay into her arms. "You worry too much. Russ is a big boy and can take care of himself. He seems very capable to me."

"You're right, of course."

Tory held Kay tightly. "If he's not back soon, we'll look for him, okay? We're not going to let anything happen to him. Just give him until the deadline. If we go rushing in there before he's due back, it'll bruise his ego. He hates me as it is."

"I don't think he hates you."

"Whatever you say."

"So you've got the evidence you need now. I guess the airport's next."

"That's right. I'll come back tomorrow and wait for the next shipments. Those two guys we heard talking confirmed there'd be shipments out of there tomorrow. I'll trail the trucks to the airport. Get a tracking device onto the plane."

"That sounds extremely dangerous. How are you planning on doing that?"

"Haven't quite figured that out yet. I may need your help."

"And what about Ron?"

"Oh, I've got some friends who will have a nice chat with him. No problem there."

At five o'clock, Russ still had not returned. Kay and Tory waited another half hour and then took off toward the mine entrance not far from where their vehicles were parked. The northern mine entrance was littered with debris and appeared abandoned. There were no signs of recent activity, no equipment stores, and no electrical lighting. The main tunnel was narrow and the timbers old and rotted. The air in the tunnel was stale and rats scattered at the sound of their footsteps.

"This is creepy beyond belief," Kay said, swiping a cobweb away from her face. "No one's been in here for years."

"Except Russ," Tory said with concern. "We need to find him and quick."

It didn't take long. About a half mile into the tunnel they hit a dead end. Speechless, they stared hopelessly at a massive wall of debris blocking their way. Old timbers, dirt, and rock had fallen, making the main tunnel inaccessible. Tory scanned the wall of debris with her flashlight and found an opening about ten feet up.

"The tunnel's not completely blocked. This cave-in looks fresh. There's a lot of loose dirt here."

Kay felt ill. "Russ. He must be on the other side. Shit, Tory. We've got to get him out of there."

"We will. You're going to stay right here."

"No way."

"Listen to me. I'm going to climb up there and shimmy through that opening. You need to stay here. If Russ is on the other side, I'm going to need your help clearing this stuff away. You'll work from this side, I'll work from the other."

"Whatever. Just hurry."

Tory wasted no time scurrying up the mountain of loose rocks and broken pieces of timber to reach the narrow opening at the top. Kay spun out of the way as rocks, pieces of timber, and coal dust fell around her. Then Tory was gone and Kay stood waiting and hoping, her heart pounding.

"Tory?" Kay gasped, trying to remain calm.

Tory's voice was muffled, but Kay heard every word. "Russ is on this side, Kay, and he's fine. Looks like a nasty bump on his head. But he's okay."

"Thank God," Kay whispered to herself. "Is it safe to start moving this stuff?" she yelled.

"From the top, Kay. We just need to widen the opening to get Russ through. Carefully and slowly start clearing from your side."

Kay went to work. Three or four times she slipped and tumbled to the ground. Her hands and arms were scraped and bleeding and she was covered from head to toe in coal dust and dirt. But every time she fell, she scrambled back up and continued to widen the opening. Finally, she crawled partway through the debris and checked the area below with her flashlight. Russ was sitting upright on the ground looking dazed and confused. Tory had ripped her shirt and tied it around Russ's forehead.

"I think you can get him through now."

"I'm going to help Russ up, Kay. When I get him to the top, grab ahold of his shoulders and pull."

"Ready when you are," Kay said, wondering how Tory was going to manage helping a man of Russ's size up a fifteen-foot wall of loose rock. It was slow going, but with incredible strength and care, Tory led Russ to the top step by step. There were several slips and each time Kay held her breath. Finally, Kay was able to reach for Russ's shoulders and pull him through. She waited for Tory to crawl through the opening and then they both helped Russ down the other side. He was mumbling under his breath, but Kay couldn't make out the words. Once they reached the floor of the tunnel, they wrapped Russ's arms around their shoulders and headed for the mine entrance as quickly as possible. Coal dust was falling all around them and the tunnel's support structure was definitely compromised. By the time they reached fresh air, they were all choking on the foul black dust.

They visited the only medical clinic in Healy; Russ's cuts and scrapes were tended to and he was finally released after an X-ray revealed no concussion. On the way back to the lodge, Russ was fully coherent and recounted what had happened in the mine.

"It was so fucking dark in there I couldn't see shit even with a flashlight. I tripped and fell into a loose beam. It gave way and I went flying. Next thing you know, I'm sittin' on the ground lookin' at a wall of dirt, coal dust, and rock."

Kay shook her head. "You were lucky."

"You can say that again. Every few minutes, some more shit would fall and I figured I was pretty much a goner. Especially since I was too dizzy to get up and try movin' that crap out of the way."

Kay pulled Russ's truck into the parking lot of the lodge. Tory, driving the Jeep, pulled in right beside them.

"How're you feeling, Russ?" Tory asked as she helped him from the truck.

"Better. You saved my life. I want to thank you."

"No thanks necessary. You'd have done the same."

"Time for you to get some rest," Kay said. "Are you hungry?"

"No. Just tired."

"We all look like hell," Tory said, grinning.

"What about our friend in the back of the truck?" Russ asked.

"When I get up to the room, I'm going to make a phone call," Tory said. "Got some buddies who are going to stop by and talk to Ronnie boy. Take him for a little ride in the country."

"They're not going to hurt him, are they?" Kay asked.

"No, not at all. Just reason with him."

As they passed through the lobby, all eyes followed them. They were covered in coal dust and mud and raised every eyebrow in the place. The desk clerk nodded with a frown and the three of them hurried onto the elevator, not wanting to risk being questioned.

In the back of her mind as Tory made love to her late that Wednesday afternoon, Kay remembered a friend saying to her once, "You never know when it's the last time you're making love to someone. That last time when things are still good or you're trying to hang on to a love that's already lost." Kay couldn't remember who had said it or what sad circumstances elicited those anguished words. She only felt that it might be true about her at that moment. After tomorrow, when Tory set out for the mines and the Healy airport, there was no way of knowing if she would ever see Tory again. That fear seemed to heighten her senses so that everything she felt was magnified a thousand times.

Tory was fucking her hard and there was a power in each thrust that made Kay surrender completely to this woman who, in many ways, was still a stranger. But the power was tempered with affection—in the gentleness of Tory's kisses, the soft caresses along Kay's legs and thighs that communicated not only desire, but love.

"Baby, you drive me crazy. I love you so much," Tory whispered.

"I love you, too," Kay answered, believing she had been pulled into a wild, hypnotic dream. Love, passion, desire had been reserved for Lela, and still this unexplainable journey had happened, was happening, and she did not want it to end.

As she came, Tory held Kay close, whispering in confusion, "You love me, too? Hearing you say that means so much."

Kay lay back, her head sinking into the pillow. She studied Tory's face—those strong jaw lines, high cheekbones, searing green eyes. Kay gently wiped the sweat from Tory's forehead and continued tracing the lines of Tory's face until she reached those soft lips. She lingered there for a moment, staring at the mouth that had kissed her passionately for the past hour. "I do love you."

"Don't want to leave you tomorrow. Don't want to leave you ever."

"Remember what you said? We're a moment in time."

"I was wrong. We're so much more than that, Kay. You know it and I know it."

"I didn't believe it until now."

"Are you tired?"

Kay laughed. "Why?"

"You know why."

"Then stop talking and kiss me again."

Early Thursday evening, Tory received a call in her room. Kay listened and realized she was talking about Ron.

"Any problems with our friend?" Tory asked. "He going to cooperate?"

When Tory hung up, Kay waited impatiently. "Well? What happened with Ron? Where is he?"

"He's in a safe place. Being taken care of. No one's hurting him. Apparently, he's not cooperating all that well. So he's going to be the government's ward for a while. Until this case is closed."

"But that could take years."

"True. But we can't risk him talking. Seems he knows more than we thought. Been listening in on phone calls at your office. His main goal was to bring you down, but he stumbled onto the mission in the process. Doesn't know all the details, but enough to make him dangerous. In the coming months, he'll live like a freakin' king. A prisoner of sorts, but a well looked after prisoner."

"Good God. What a mess."

"Can't blame yourself for his stupidity."

"No. But it's another troublesome wrinkle."

"You'll need to tell Connie Huntington that Ron quit. Never came back to work. Won't be an unbelievable story since he was disgruntled to begin with."

"Swell. Another lie I have to tell."

At two o'clock Thursday morning, Russ and Kay sat in Russ's truck outside the gates of the Healy airport waiting for a call from Tory on Kay's cell phone. At midnight, Tory drove to Trapper Creek, hoping to catch the next shipment of yellowcake out of the mine. The plan was for Tory to call ahead when the trucks left with the shipment. Russ and Kay were to wait for the trucks and follow them to the hangar that was being used to unload the yellowcake. With their government-issue IDs, they obtained a list of the private hangars from airport security. All were located at the northern end of the airport and were used to house private jets. The jets were all Lear and had a maximum flying range of about two thousand miles before having to refuel, making flights over the U.S. border into Canada a distinct possibility. As they sat in the truck waiting for Tory, Kay studied a map of North America. A Lear jet could easily fly as far as Saskatchewan before having to touch down. Switching planes or simply refueling could get the shipment to Montreal in as little as eight hours.

"What's keepin' her?" Russ wondered aloud while punching buttons on the radio.

Kay folded the map and peered out the window. "I don't know, but I'm starting to worry. She should've called by this time."

"So you in love with her?"

"Yes, but it hardly matters. She's going to Montreal to finish this case and I'm going back to Anchorage to pick up where I left off with my life. I'll probably never see her again."

"You think you can just do that?"

"What?"

"Pick up where you left off?"

"What else can I do?"

"Come clean."

"I could do that. In fact, I would do that, if it weren't for the fact that Tory doesn't exist. I can't say a word about her to anyone. Nothing about this trip to Sugarloaf ever happened."

"Makes it kinda easy, don't it?"

"That's insensitive. It's not going to be easy. I may not be able to come clean, to use your words. But I still have to live with myself and how I feel about Tory. How I feel about Lela."

The cell phone rang. "Hey, babe," Tory said when Kay answered. "The trucks are on their way."

"We were getting worried, Tory. Where are you?"

"On my way to you. Watch for two Eagle Pass Coal Mining trucks. Russ was right about that—they're using those trucks as a cover. Russ knows what they look like so they won't be hard to spot. Besides, there's not much traffic at this ungodly hour of the night. Find out which hangar they head to. Okay?"

"Okay."

"See you soon."

About twenty minutes later, two Eagle Pass Coal Mining trucks pulled onto the airport access road. Russ and Kay waited for the trucks to pass and then rolled out of the parking lot with headlights off. They hung back about ten car lengths, following them to a turnoff where three private hangars were located. Russ swung the truck to the side of the road. A short time later, Kay and Russ observed the two trucks parking alongside the middle hangar. Four shadowy figures disappeared into the hangar, telling Kay and Russ everything they needed to know. Russ turned the truck, heading back to the airport parking lot, where they found Tory waiting in the park service Jeep.

"Middle hangar, north access road," Kay said, leaning into the Jeep's window.

Tory smiled and patted her arm. "Thanks, babe. Gotta go do my thing. See you back at the lodge." Tory looked at her watch. "Meet you in the lobby in one hour."

"Hope she knows what she's doin'," Russ half-mumbled as he sped down the main road from the airport. "She's on her own now."

Kay and Russ waited in the lobby. Pacing back and forth, Kay wrung her hands while Russ sat on a nearby sofa, following her with his eyes. Russ couldn't stand it anymore.

"Kay, take a load off. You're makin' me nervous and I ain't that fond of her."

"Sorry. But we've come so far. I just want her to plant the tracking device on that damned jet so the CIA can follow it and put an end to this madness."

"She'll be fine. She annoys the crap out of me, but she's good at what she does."

"I'm surprised to hear you say that."

"I can give credit where credit's due."

Another forty-five minutes passed before Tory returned. She walked into the lobby from the street with that trademark grin, her hair slightly damp from a light rain that had begun to fall.

"Everything okay?" Kay asked anxiously.

"Fine. Let's find a place where we can talk."

They strolled outside, standing at the end of the dimly lit parking lot. It was about four-thirty in the morning and the sun was inching over the horizon, flooding the sky with an orange-red glow. The only sound was the rain pelting their windbreakers. Tory smoked, not knowing what to say, and Russ chewed on some Slim Jims. Kay stood quietly staring at the sidewalk, understanding that they had reached the end.

Tory glanced at her watch. "A helicopter's picking me up in an hour at the airport. It's already been verified that the tracking device is working. The Lear jet's headed for Canada, just as we suspected. I've got to go find out where. My job's not over yet, but yours is. I can't thank you both enough. Couldn't have gotten this far without you."

"Heck, we didn't do nothin'," Russ said. "We just followed your lead," he added graciously. He extended his hand and Tory accepted the gesture. "You and Kay are gonna wanna talk, so I'll leave you to it. Good luck, Tory. You saved my ass back in that mine. Crawlin' through that hole to find me was gutsy. I gotta thank you again for that."

"My pleasure, Russ."

Russ turned to Kay. "I guess you'll be givin' Tory a ride to the airport?"

"Yeah. I will."

"See you later then."

Russ lumbered down the sidewalk to the lobby entrance. At the door, he turned and smiled, giving Tory a mock salute. Tory waved and smiled, then turned to Kay. "Ready to go?"

"Sure. But only if you drive. Wouldn't be right for me to take the wheel of that Jeep now."

Tory laughed and took Kay's arm. "No, I guess not."

At the airport they had half an hour to kill. They sat in the Jeep holding hands, neither knowing what to say. Kay tried to swallow the feelings that were balled up in her throat. She understood without question that she would probably never see Tory again.

Turning toward Kay, Tory held her hands. "Kay, if things were different, if I didn't have to leave, what do you think would happen with us?"

"I don't know."

"I do," Tory answered, kissing Kay's cheek. "We'd go back to Anchorage and talk to Lela. We'd tell her as best we could that we fell in love and that it wasn't planned, but that these things happen to people. Not by design. Not because we wanted to hurt anyone. Just because." Tory put her arms around Kay and pulled her close.

"Then we'd take care of Alex, make sure she was well and happy and settled. And when we could, when the time was right, we'd find that fishing village I talked about. Remember? And we'd live in a small house, nothing fancy, right by the creek or lake or stream. At night, we'd listen to the water running just outside the bedroom window. In the winter, we'd watch the snow fall huddled by the living room fireplace, covered in afghans, drinking a beer. Sound good?"

"For a dream, yes."

Nervously, Tory checked her watch. "Almost time to go." Cupping Kay's face, Tory kissed her gently—then deeply with a Tory-like insistence that lingered long after the kiss ended. The next thing Kay knew, her hand was in Tory's as they ran across the tarmac toward the helicopter. About twenty feet shy of the swirling rotor blades, Tory stopped. She let go of Kay's hand and said, "I love you, Kay Westmore. Like I've never loved anyone else."

"I love you, too."

"Bye babe." Tory wrapped her arms around Kay and hugged her tightly, kissing her lightly on the forehead. Then she ran for the helicopter, ducking as she neared the open cockpit. She turned one last time and yelled over the roar of the engine. Kay strained to hear and was barely able to make out the words. "I love you, Kay. I never thought I'd fall in love. And that's why I'm coming back for you. You hear me, babe? I will be back for you."

Kay stood for a long time watching the helicopter disappear into the early morning sky. Tears streamed down her face and she was unable to move. For minutes that seemed like hours she stood motionless, staring at an empty sky that was no match for the emptiness within.

Window shades completely drawn, Kay sat in the darkness of her hotel room Friday afternoon staring at the ceiling. Tory's final words echoed again and again inside her head. When it was all over, Tory was coming back. Kay remembered Tory saying that she trained all of her life for one mission and that this was that one mission. A rogue lying in wait for a phone call and one job. When that job was over Tory would go back to being whoever she was before—a person Kay didn't even know.

Kay punched the numbers on her phone. Within minutes, she connected to Grace Perry's home number.

"Kay, what the hell's going on?"

Grace sounded furious, as usual. But for once it didn't bother Kay. "The agent Russ and I were working with instructed me to call you only when our work was done. It's done now."

"I'll see you in Anchorage for a full report on Wednesday. I'd be there sooner, but I've got some senators breathing down my neck. Remember them?"

"I do."

"Where is our agent friend now?"

"I'd rather not say over the open phone line."

Grace sighed her impatience into the phone. "Very well. Wednesday at nine o'clock sharp. I'll be in your office."

Chapter Seven

It was Saturday afternoon and the sun was warm, the sky a brilliant blue. The view of the mountains behind the house was clear and vibrant, as though she could reach out and touch the cool mountain snow. Kay sat in the driveway of her home composing herself, wondering what she could possibly do to allay the guilt she felt, to hide the changes that had taken place inside her heart during the past two weeks. During the drive back from Healy, she tried to rationalize the choices she had made, like some criminal who enters a plea of temporary insanity. The bizarre events at Sugarloaf and Riley Creek were dreamlike, causing her to question if Tory Mitchell ever existed.

Stepping inside the front door, Kay dropped her backpack in the foyer. It was quiet and she wondered if anyone was home. She walked through the kitchen toward the patio. The French doors were open to the cool afternoon air where Al lounged in the chaise reading the newspaper. Lela was probably at work, and Kay was relieved.

"Hey, babe. Look who's home."

Al dropped the paper and jumped up from the chair into Kay's arms. "Kay! Oh my God, we've missed you so much. How are you?" Al stood back and looked at Kay with eyes as blue as the sky above them. "You look a little tired. You must be thrilled to be home."

"I am. And tired, too. It's been a long two weeks. Russ and I didn't finish half of what we set out to do. The rain disrupted the entire schedule."

"You mean the monsoon. It's been depressing to say the least."

"How are you, Al?"

"Fine. Finished the chemotherapy last week. Still a bit worn out. But knowing it was the last time really got me through it."

"Sorry I wasn't here for you."

"Don't be silly. You've been here for the past seven months."

Kay threw her arms around Al's shoulders and hung on for dear life. She choked back tears and struggled for control.

"Kay, sweetheart, are you all right?"

"Yeah. I just want to hold you."

"I'm fine, Kay. Really."

Kay finally let go and studied Al's face. "You look like a million. You're right. I'm thrilled to be home."

"Hungry?"

"Not really. But if you're planning something for dinner, I'm sure I can summon an appetite. After two weeks of Slim Jims and trail mix, I'm ready for real food."

"I think I can manage something. Lela returned from Juneau yesterday. She's at the Anchorage office today and should be home in a couple of hours. We can celebrate your homecoming and the end of my chemotherapy."

"Great. I think I'll lie down for a while if you don't mind."

"Not at all. You sure you're okay? You seem depressed or something."

"Just tired."

She was dreaming and she knew it. Someone spoke her name—over and over again. But it was like listening to a voice through someone else's ears—muffled and far away. She ran toward the sound—up and down shadowy streets, rain stinging her face, a cold wind at her back. The sound of the voice echoed from street to street until she came to a cobblestone square with a fountain carved from mountain stone. The spray of the fountain mixed with the rain, cold as glacier ice. Suddenly, she felt an aura of love surrounding her. The voice was finally clear, distinct, familiar. Yes, she recognized the voice calling her name, knew who it belonged to before the attractive silhouette emerged from the shadows, before she caught a glimpse of the half-smile and heard approaching footsteps, boots scraping across stone. She watched in silence as a hand ruffled hair already matted by the rain, listened as the voice cracked with emotion, stumbling over her name again before the final words came, "I love you, Kay."

The ceiling came in and out of focus. Fatigue confused her as Kay struggled to assimilate her surroundings. She remembered the dream, but the visage of the person who emerged from the dream's shadows was indistinct now, clouded by those first few waking moments. She closed her eyes again, wanting to summon the sound of the voice, the outline of the woman who had stood at the center of everything in that driving rain. But she was gone and only the starkness of what was real remained.

Kay felt a hand on her arm and she jumped.

"My beautiful Kay. You are finally home."

Lela's lips were as soft as the edges of that dream and Kay lingered over the kiss. "I missed you."

"My heart is full again. I have been thinking about nothing but us for these last two weeks."

Kay bit her lip, forcing guilt back with the memories of Tory. "We've disconnected somewhere, somehow."

"I know, darling. And I fear it has been my fault. Too much work. It is not as important as us."

"You're not entirely to blame. Circumstances, Lela. Both jobs. Al getting sick. My father dying. All of it's been too much."

"But we are strong, Kay."

"I've tried to be strong. It's what everyone expects of me."

Kay spent the weekend in a daze, going through the motions with Lela and Al, wandering through the house, roaming the property, walking the shores of Cook Inlet alone, searching for the part of her she left behind in the mines under the Sugarloaf Valley. She was convinced that the answer was in the dream she had the day she returned home. But as the days passed, the dream faded, taking with it the two weeks with Tory until those moments seemed like another lifetime. The one intact memory was Tory's voice rising above the violent whir of helicopter blades, "I will be back for you."

The first two days at the office were strange. There was no other word to describe it. Russ and Kay barely spoke and Tammy seemed intent on finding out what happened at Sugarloaf.

"Did you guys have a fight or something?" she asked Kay on Tuesday morning.

Kay swallowed the last bite of a jelly doughnut and raised her eyebrows at Tammy. "What makes you think that?"

"You've got to be kidding. I may be younger than both of you, but I'm not stupid. You're both walking around here like you got your bodies snatched. You ever see that old movie?"

"*The Invasion of the Body Snatchers?*" Kay asked.

"Yeah. You two are like the pods in that movie—like you got the life sucked out of you when you were on that trip."

"Is it that bad?"

"Worse. So what the hell happened?" Tammy ripped open two packets of sugar and mixed them into her coffee. "Has something to do with that agent, doesn't it?"

"You're far too inquisitive."

"Maybe. But I'd like to see the old Kay and Russ back. I used to have fun working here." Tammy shrugged and shook her head. "Besides, I'm worried about you guys."

"Well, you're absolutely right. Enough is enough. No more worries. Everything's going to be fine."

Kay knocked softly on Russ's door. She heard a grunt and accepted that as a signal to enter. "Hey, how's it going?" she asked while fiddling with the loose doorknob.

"Okay. Need somethin'?"

"Can I come in and sit down for a minute?"

"Knock yourself out."

Kay sat down and said, "That may not be a bad idea."

Russ pushed himself away from the computer and swiveled around to face Kay. "Say what?"

"Knock myself out. Not a bad idea. I've sure made a mess of things and maybe taking a hammer to my skull's not a bad idea. Might knock some sense into me."

"Yeah, maybe. But you'll have to pass the hammer over when you're done. I could use a whack in the head myself."

"The past couple of months have been a bitch. I've got all kinds of excuses. Al getting sick, my Dad dying. No time with Lela. But I'm so sick of making excuses—of lying to everyone, including myself."

"Who you gonna talk to but me? We ain't supposed to say nothin' about Sugarloaf or what we were doin' there."

"Actually, I've been talking to myself a lot. Walking down at the inlet having a running conversation with myself. The inside of my head is sick of listening to me."

"You can talk to me, Kay. All that stuff we said—that was just 'cause we were stressed out. Both of us."

"Tammy thinks we've been body-snatched."

For the first time in days, Russ laughed. It was the best sound in the world. "She may be right. It kinda feels that way."

"Can we talk for a moment as friends? Not boss and employee, but as friends?"

"Only if you promise not to nag me."

"When have I ever done that?" Kay quickly held up her hand. "Never mind. Don't answer that question."

"I won't."

"As your friend, I just want to say how much I love you and how sorry I am about everything. I know I've disappointed you and that hurts."

Russ stroked his beard and struggled for composure. "No more than I've disappointed and hurt you. Don't know what's gonna happen, Kay. But I do know that I can't imagine my life without you as a friend."

"And as a boss?"

"Do we hafta go there?"

They both laughed. Russ reached across the desk and squeezed Kay's hand. No more words were necessary.

When Grace Perry arrived on Wednesday and gave Kay a look that only Grace could manage—a look that said, "All is not well"— Kay immediately forgot the warm fuzzies she and Russ summoned back into the office the day before. Grace was clearly frazzled, and that observation alone set Kay back on her heels. It was unlike Grace to let anything unnerve her to the point where she fidgeted endlessly, digging around in her briefcase and playing with her cell phone. Kay braced herself by sitting on her hands, not wanting to show her own nervousness.

"What is it, Grace?"

With a look of disgust, Grace threw the cell phone into her briefcase. "I'm sorry to have telegraphed my mood. But I have some unpleasant news."

"What?"

"First, while we've shut down the illegal mining operation under Sugarloaf, we've been unable to track all of those involved. We don't know if the Egyptian government was providing cover to the operatives in Cairo or even if the Canadian government was involved since the core of the operation was traced to Montreal. This case will be open for years and may never be resolved."

"But no more illegal yellowcake shipments out of Alaska."

"That much we can be happy about. Whoever the operatives are, they have no more yellowcake to sell to rogue nations. However, the agent you and Russ worked with for the past two weeks is dead."

Kay flinched as though she'd been kicked in the gut. She thought she was going to be sick. "I don't believe it."

"I'm sorry. I know it must be hard to hear this news about someone you worked with under difficult circumstances."

"Difficult circumstances? Tory Mitchell saved our lives. Both mine and Russ's. What happened?"

"I don't know, Kay. They wouldn't provide any details."

"Who are *they*?"

"The CIA. I'm truly sorry."

Kay dropped her head into her hands. Tears came and she couldn't stop them. "I have to go, Grace. I'm sorry. Can we talk tomorrow?"

"Kay, I had no idea this news would be such a heavy blow. I mean, it must be awful to hear this about someone you met and worked with. I just didn't think that after only two weeks you'd . . ."

"Care about her? She saved our lives, Grace. It's hard to dismiss something like that."

"Of course it is. I'll be in town until the end of the week." Grace got up and put a hand on Kay's shoulder. "I'll see you tomorrow morning."

A few days later, Grace left for Washington. At work things returned to normal—at least on the surface. Russ was still shaken by the news of Tory's death and retreated to his office. Kay also retreated, lost in the memories of the woman who had so quickly and completely impacted her life.

Finally, three weeks after Grace's stunning news, when she couldn't stand it any longer, Kay picked up the phone and began working through Grace and her contacts at the CIA to obtain more information about Tory—when and how she died, where she had been buried. No less than fifty phone calls and countless dead ends later, Kay was completely frustrated and angry. Grace suddenly became more evasive and stingy with information. Her own phone calls to the CIA, NSA, and FBI were ignored. At one point, Kay suspected her phone was being tapped. Announcing to her staff and her boss that she was taking a vacation, Kay purchased a round-trip airline ticket. She told Lela and Al she was leaving town on business, packed her bags, and drove to the Anchorage airport.

It was a sunny, clear summer day in Portland, Maine. A stiff Atlantic breeze blew her hair across her face as she strode up the driveway of the red brick colonial that rested on a bluff not far from the rocky beaches below. When the door opened, she saw the image of Tory—the strong features and deep green eyes recognizable in Colonel Mitchell's face. The resemblance of father and daughter was dramatic and Kay struggled to remain composed.

"Colonel Mitchell, I'm Kay Westmore. We spoke several times on the phone."

"Kay, we finally meet. Please come in."

The den was filled with Air Force memorabilia from Colonel Mitchell's long and illustrious career as a pilot and Air Force commander. Retired now, he still conducted research for the military's Special Forces division. Leaning back in his chair behind a large mahogany desk, the Colonel stared at Kay intently. His dark hair, chiseled features, and deep green eyes were mesmerizing.

"You look so much like your daughter, Colonel."

"I've often been told that. Thank you. You've gone to a lot of trouble inquiring about my daughter's death. Perhaps now you'll tell me why."

"As I explained by phone, I worked with your daughter on her last mission. Her death came as a deep shock to me. Even though I only knew Tory for fourteen days, I cared very much for her. She also saved my life and the life of my colleague."

"I see," the Colonel said, clasping his hands across his waist. "And so you've come to learn more about her and to pay your last respects?"

"Yes, sir. That's correct."

"My daughter meant the world to me. She was my only child and her death is a staggering blow. I haven't been completely and adequately informed about the circumstances surrounding Tory's death. Oh, I've been told things. But I've served this government long enough to understand that when the CIA is involved, some details may remain sealed forever. I've been working every day to get my hands on some of the classified documents related to the case."

"I've been doing the same. No luck. I've started to question whom I can trust. That's another reason I'm here."

"Understood. We'll talk more about that later."

"I know this is a painful question to answer, but do you know how Tory died? I haven't been able to find out."

"The only information I was given is that Tory died somewhere in Canada. In some kind of explosion."

"Explosion?"

"Yes." Colonel Mitchell hung his head, his face deeply etched in sorrow. "Tory's body was burnt beyond recognition. Her mother and I received the remains here and buried her in Portland."

"Again, I'm so sorry for your loss."

"Will you join my wife and me for dinner? We'd like to hear about the last two weeks of our daughter's life."

"Of course."

"After dinner, I'll drive you to the cemetery if that's something you'd like to do."

"Yes. I very much want to pay my respects."

"Tory meant a lot to you. I can see that."

"She did. I feel as though I knew her a lot longer than two weeks. Tory was strong, genuine, courageous. She was the kind of person that makes an immediate impact."

"That was my daughter. She could fill a room with her presence. This house feels very empty now."

The sun was just beginning to set, casting a tawny glow across the carefully manicured grass where Kay stood, eyes closed, trying to summon the memories of recent weeks. Tory's father had returned to the car, leaving her alone. There was a temporary marker with Tory's name, date of birth, and date of death in raised bronze letters. Kay stooped to touch the cold plaque, her fingers tracing the letters that spelled TORY. Emotions came in a wave—loss, anger, guilt. "You promised you'd come back for me," Kay whispered. "You promised, and now somehow I have to go on without you. I'll always love you. Always be grateful." Kay stood, wiping away the tears that stung her cheeks. "I'll find out who did this, Tory. I don't know how. It may take months, even years. But that's my promise to you. And when I finally know what happened, I will be back."

The August evening air was cool. A week after her visit to Portland, Kay sat on the deck behind her home watching an eagle soar toward the mountain ridge, riding an invisible air current, wings motionless as its silhouette glided toward the horizon. It had been a difficult week. She concentrated on work at the office and then stayed late into the evenings making phone calls to Washington—trying to get information on Tory's final hours, where and how she had died. Colonel Mitchell also continued to investigate his daughter's death and Kay kept in close contact with him. They shared the small scraps of information they were able to unearth from beneath mounds of red tape and government secrecy. Surprisingly, Grace Perry offered her help by promising to tap in to connections in the Senate. So far, nothing had broken open—at least according to Grace. But Kay was convinced that Grace knew much more than she was willing or able to reveal and that her only reason for offering Kay her help was to keep tabs on her. A trust gap developed between Kay and Grace, and Kay felt uneasy and on edge whenever they spoke. Something had drastically changed, but that something remained shrouded by Tory's death. And now, more than ever, the road to finding out who murdered Tory seemed long and difficult.

Lela sat to her right, sipping a glass of wine. "You seem as far away as that eagle," she said suddenly. "I wonder where you have been these last weeks."

"I'm sorry. I guess it's my turn to be distracted with work."

"I think it must be something else. There is a wound to your heart that is new. I can feel it."

"It's stress and worry. About us, work, Al. I think it's finally taken a toll." Kay blinked tears away. She hated lying to Lela. But she had also made a promise to herself that when she found out what happened to Tory, she would work to get the CIA records declassified so she could finally tell Lela the truth. That she loved her, but had also loved Tory. She understood what the consequences might be—that Lela might leave her. Or forgive her. That their relationship might be destroyed. Or healed. Kay glanced toward the heavens. The eagle was a speck on the horizon now, soaring closer to the mountains. Its powerful wings seemed to embrace the highest peak. Lela reached for Kay's hand. Kay accepted Lela's hand into her own and held on tightly, knowing now, more than ever, just how fragile love is.